Strong arms gripped Annie's shoulders.

"What do you think you're doing? Are you trying to get yourself killed?"

Annie felt the hot splash of tears on her cheeks. "I can't stand by and watch it all go up in smoke. My whole life is in there!" She let out a plaintive howl. She saw his ice-blue eyes widen. A muscle in his jaw began to twitch. He released her shoulders and pivoted around so that he was facing the plane.

Turning back toward her, he yelled, "Get out of this area as fast as you can. Run as far as you can upwind. Now!" She watched as he rushed toward the plane, wrenched open the cargo hold and yanked her suitcases out in one fluid motion. With an amazing display of agility, he ran back toward her at breakneck speed. One look at his expression and Annie began to run in the opposite direction as fast as she could.

A thunderous noise interrupted the silence. A deafening roar rent the air.

Belle Calhoune grew up in a small town in Massachusetts. Married to her college sweetheart, she is raising two lovely daughters in Connecticut. A dog lover, she has one mini poodle and a chocolate Lab. Writing for the Love Inspired line is a dream come true. Working at home in her pajamas is one of the best perks of the job. Belle enjoys summers in Cape Cod, traveling and reading.

Books by Belle Calhoune

Love Inspired

Alaskan Grooms

An Alaskan Wedding
Alaskan Reunion
A Match Made in Alaska

Reunited with the Sheriff
Forever Her Hero
Heart of a Soldier

A Match
Made in Alaska

Belle Calhoune

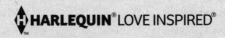

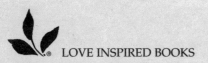

LOVE INSPIRED BOOKS

Recycling programs
for this product may
not exist in your area.

ISBN-13: 978-0-373-71968-6

A Match Made in Alaska

www.Harlequin.com

Printed in U.S.A.

"There is no fear in love; but perfect love casteth out fear: because fear hath torment. He that feareth is not made perfect in love."
—*1 John* 4:18

This book is dedicated to my own Annie…
my mother, Dr. Anne Murray Bell.
Not a day goes by that I don't miss you.

Acknowledgments

A huge thank you to my editor, Emily Rodmell,
for her unwavering support for Love, Alaska.
And for keeping me on course.

I am very thankful for all the readers
who have written to me and asked about
future stories set in Love, Alaska.

A special thanks to Bob Moore
for all his expertise on aviation.

Chapter One

"Welcome to O'Rourke Charters. Thank you for choosing to fly with us today. Why don't you make yourself comfortable for the flight, Miss Murray?" Pilot Declan O'Rourke waved Annie Murray toward her seat on the small plane. As she walked past him, he looked down at her leopard pajama pants and slightly shook his head, unable to hide his grin.

"Thank you," Annie said in her cheeriest voice, determined to be positive. "I'm happy to be here." She took a good look at him, hoping he didn't consider her perusal staring. This Alaskan pilot was a very impressive-looking man. She hadn't expected him to be quite so rugged and handsome.

He was tall, hovering at six foot three or so, she imagined, with an athletic, lean build. He was wearing a beat-up leather aviator jacket and a pair of jeans. His face was the real standout. Cheekbones for days and a perfectly symmetrical face. He had sea-blue eyes and a head of blond hair. A strong jaw completed the picture.

"Don't forget your headset," he reminded her, holding out one for her.

Annie settled into her seat on the seaplane and let out a tremendous sigh as she looked around her. She hadn't imagined being the sole passenger on the flight, although the plane wasn't big enough to accommodate more than a few people. Really teeny-tiny, she realized. Why hadn't she thought about her tendency toward claustrophobia? She wasn't afraid of flying, but up till this point in time, the planes had always been normal-size ones.

Keep your eye on the prize. Gram's voice buzzed in her ears. A little discomfort was worth it if she found her one true love.

At the moment she was thankful for small blessings. Her earlier flight from Bangor, Maine, had been almost two hours late landing at the Anchorage International Airport. In order to make her connecting flight to the small fishing village, she had raced from one terminal all the way to the farthest part of the airport. Declan O'Rourke had been impatiently waiting for her arrival at the terminal. As owner of O'Rourke Charters, he was the pilot she had hired, sight unseen, to fly her to Love.

As the plane took off and began to climb gradually in altitude, Annie closed her Leslie Lemon mystery novel and peered out the window at the stunning Alaskan landscape. It was awe inspiring. She grinned at the sight of snow-dusted mountains looming in the distance. It felt like a whole new world, light-years away from her life in New England. She was now on her way to her final destination—Love, Alaska. The plane was soaring somewhere above Anchorage, and in less than an hour they would arrive in Love.

Love, Alaska, was a town filled with hot bachelors looking for love. And thankfully for her, there was a shortage of single women in the fishing village. It was leaps and bounds away from the situation she was leaving behind in Maine. Whimsy was filled with senior citizens. Eligible men were as elusive in her hometown as a Bigfoot sighting. Her chances of being struck by lightning were far greater than being in a serious relationship in her hometown. Words couldn't express how much she wanted to find that special someone and walk down the aisle. So now she was headed to Love in order to find her own happily-ever-after. The cherry on top was that she had been hired as head librarian for the newly restored Free Library of Love.

And, although she hadn't confided in a single person about her quest, she was hoping to find the missing pieces of her family puzzle in the Alaskan hamlet. Discovering the identity of her grandfather was high on her agenda. Maybe if she was able to locate her long-lost family members, she would find peace and welcoming arms. Life had been pretty lonely lately.

"How's everything back there?" The pilot's voice came through the headset. Loud rumblings from the cockpit would have made it impossible for them to communicate without the gear. Annie was aware that pilots also wore headphones to spare themselves from hearing loss.

"Everything is fine," she answered. "I'm enjoying the beautiful scenery."

She swung her gaze toward the cockpit, where the impossibly handsome pilot was handling the controls with an authoritative air. Prior to hiring Mr. O'Rourke, she had looked into his background and discovered that he was a seasoned pilot who had earned rave reviews for his expertise and skill. However, her extensive research hadn't prepared her for coming face-to-face with the most eye-catching man she had ever laid eyes on.

It sort of made sense. She'd seen photos in a magazine of some of the men from this lovelorn town. They weren't as handsome as Declan O'Rourke, but they were cut from the same cloth. Good-looking, Alaskan eye candy. It was a major selling point for Operation Love, a program that matched up single women across the United States with the bachelors in Love. And women from all around the United States seemed to be paying attention.

Despite his jaw-dropping looks, he wasn't exactly warm and fuzzy. His first glance in her direction had been comprised of a raised eyebrow and a frown. Humph! Hadn't he ever seen a person in fuzzy leopard pants before? She'd worn the pajama pants so she could be comfortable during the seven-and-a-half-hour flight from Maine. Due to unexpected turbulence, she hadn't been able to change out of her comfy pants as she'd planned. So, instead of looking sophisticated and sharp, she looked downright peculiar.

It didn't matter what other people thought about her. Or at least, it shouldn't. Part of this grand adventure meant ridding herself of old insecurities and doubts. Traveling to Love as part of Mayor Jasper Prescott's Operation Love campaign meant that after so many years of having her nose stuck in a book, she was finally taking steps toward living the life she'd always imagined.

As the plane flew across the Alaskan tundra,

Annie surveyed the vast landscape stretched out before her. Goose bumps rose on her arms. She had always dreamed of seeing Alaska in person rather than reading about it in travel books and encyclopedias. Fat clouds resembled cotton candy as the sun bounced off them. The ground below was powdered with white snow. It almost resembled spun sugar, like the cupcakes at Mabel's Cupcake Haven back home. She felt a stab of homesickness. Mabel's cupcakes had always been Gram's favorite.

Just thinking about her sweet Gram caused a lump to form in her throat. She was the only person in her life who had ever shown her unconditional love and acceptance. And now that she had passed away, Annie felt as if she needed to do something in memory of Aurelia Alice Murray, the woman who had raised her and taught her everything she knew about life and love and faith. The ache of loss never truly went away. It had lessened with time, but it was still there—a painful reminder that a huge chunk of her heart was now missing.

"We should be arriving in Love right on schedule. Sit back and enjoy the flight, Miss Murray," Mr. O'Rourke announced, turning around and flashing her a megawatt smile that did funny things to her stomach. A host of butterflies was now fluttering low in her belly. Her pulse was racing.

Men like him were used to charming women like her. He had charisma. One smile was probably all it took, she surmised. He could be as grumpy as a bear and then, as long as he turned on his pearly smile, all would be forgiven. She let out a sigh. Gorgeous men like Declan O'Rourke were ones she intended to steer clear of in her quest for romance. She knew from Gram, her mother and her own experiences with love that good-looking charmers led women on a path straight to heartache.

A short while later, her thoughts were interrupted by another comment from the pilot. "If you look out the left side of the plane, you can see a glacier," he called out. "It's pretty famous in these parts. We Alaskans think it's pretty spectacular."

Annie sucked in a breath at the sight of the glacier. It was breathtaking even from this distance. "It's gorgeous!" she said, feeling awestruck by the rivers of ice below.

Anticipation was beginning to build up inside her as the minutes passed. A quick glance at her watch revealed that they were almost halfway through the flight. Love, Alaska, was within reach. For so long now, Gram's stories had fueled her curiosity about the Alaskan hamlet where her grandmother had been born and raised. As a child, she had often fantasized about how amazing it would have been if they had lived in the small fishing village. All of these years, she'd had to be content with imagining the town of Love. Now she would actually be able to live in it. She couldn't wait to become a part of the tight-knit community and to walk along the same steps Gram had traveled.

No one is ever a stranger for long in Love. Gram's voice surrounded her, providing all the comfort of one of her knitted blankets. Her grandmother had always taken such pride in her knitting. Each project had been made with love. Tears pricked her eyes as memories washed over her like a strong tide. The loss was still a sharp wound in her heart. Grief was like an ocean, adventure was going to end? All she had wanted to do in making this voyage was to chase after her dreams. Instead she was going to plummet to her death in a rinky-dink toy plane. Maybe she should never have left Whimsy in the first place. At least there she might have had an opportunity to die of old age in her bed.

Dear Lord, please don't let this be the end. Even though things have been a little rough lately, I love being alive. And I have so much more living to do. I want to fall in love. I want to become a mother. I want to make a difference in this world. And I want to change people's lives with the gift of books. Mercy, Lord. Above all else, mercy.

She shut her eyes tightly as the plane continued to drop out of the sky. Her stomach lurched as she felt the seaplane nose-dive toward the snow-covered ground at an alarming speed. If these were her last moments on earth and God was calling her home, she would handle it with grace and courage. She would accept His will.

The plane hit the ground with a thunderous bang, then veered to the right before skidding for an agonizing amount of time. It finally came to a grinding halt. They had crash-landed! As the plane seemed to crumple all around her, Annie let out a blood-curdling scream that she felt certain could be heard all the way back in Maine.

Declan O'Rourke had been flying planes since he was fourteen years old. He knew them inside and out. It was pretty much the only legacy his old man had ever handed down to him. His father had also been a pilot until he had thrown it all away and become a felon. His grandfather had given him a vast knowledge ebbing and flowing and rising up without warning. She swiped away her tears with the back of her hand, reminding herself that Gram would have been thrilled by Annie's decision to relocate to her beloved hometown. They had often talked about one day taking a trip to the place of Gram's birth. The car accident that had ended her grandmother's life short-circuited those plans. Annie would always regret not having made the trip to Love with the woman who had raised her.

"Is this your first time in Alaska?" The rich timbre of Mr. O'Rourke's voice trickled through the headset. "If so, you're in for a treat. There's no finer state than the last frontier."

"Yes. I'm a first-timer," she answered. "But it's something I've dreamed of doing my whole life."

"Well, I'm happy to be able to help you check something off your bucket list." His voice was infused with merriment. She wasn't certain if he was laughing with her or at her.

Through the headset, she could hear him singing a song that had been really popular a few years ago about love gone wrong. His voice wasn't half-bad, Annie thought. It took a confident man to sing like that at the top of his lungs.

She gazed out the window and allowed herself to daydream for a moment. Nottingham Woods. Deer Run Lake. The shops on Jarvis Street. Kachemak Bay. Pretty soon Annie would be seeing all of these local landmarks for herself. And she would enjoy every moment of exploring her new world. All in loving memory of Gram, the woman who had shown her unconditional love and encouraged her to fly like an eagle. Although she was proud of her profession as of the inner workings of planes and how to be a first-class pilot. He had given Declan something in his life to be proud of achieving. He'd flown in snowstorms, rainstorms and through ice and hail, thunder, lightning and dense fog. On one occasion he had guided his plane without the use of instruments when they had failed him. Not once had he ever been faced with an emergency crash landing. There had been instances when things had gotten dicey, but nothing like this moment in which he had landed the plane with white knuckles gripping the controls.

He held out his hands in front of him. They were shaking uncontrollably.

Once he'd collected himself, he took a moment to utter a prayer of thanks to the big guy upstairs. God had shown him mercy in a terrifying situation. In those moments of stark fear, God had been at his side, guiding him to safety. He quickly got up from his seat and left the cockpit. On his way out, he grabbed the emergency kit he had stashed nearby. He didn't have a moment to spare. Even though he was still in shock, he needed to assume control of the situation. As the pilot of this aircraft, he was responsible for Miss Murray. He needed to ensure that she made it safely out of the plane. And judging by the way she'd just screamed, she was alive and kicking.

When he reached the back of the plane, he noticed his passenger was sitting in her seat with her eyes pressed closed. Part of the infrastructure of the plane had collapsed around her. He leaned down so that his face was near hers. "Miss Murray. Are you all right?"

"Are we alive?" Annie's eyelids didn't even flutter. She was sitting in her seat, ramrod straight, her hands clutching the armrest. She wasn't moving a muscle. But he did a quick perusal of her and thought she hadn't sustained any injuries.

Despite the grave circumstances, her question made him want to laugh. "I can assure you that we are very much alive, Miss Murray."

"Thank You, Lord," she whispered. "I'm going to spend the rest of my life living up to Your faith in me."

A protective instinct rose up inside him. He squashed the urge to put his arm around her and tell her everything was going to be all right. For starters, he had never been in a plane crash, and he had no idea whether they were going to make it through this ordeal. The one thing he did know for certain was that they needed to exit the plane quickly. He could smell smoke, although he couldn't see any flames yet.

"Miss Murray, we need to get off the plane in case there's an explosion from the fuel."

Her eyes flew open upon hearing his words. They were a pretty brown with caramel flecks. Without her oversize glasses weighing her down, she was actually pretty cute. She had a button nose and shoulder-length glossy hair. A few freckles were scattered across the bridge of her nose.

Her glasses? They were no longer on her face. Had they flown off in the crash? He looked around for a moment, feeling a stab of dismay when he spotted them on the floor next to her seat, smashed to smithereens. Declan picked them up and brushed them off against his jacket. He poked out the remaining bits of glass, leaving just the frame intact. It was better than nothing, he supposed, although he surmised the glasses were a total loss.

"I hate to tell you, but your glasses are shattered."
Declan reluctantly held out the broken eyeglasses.

She reached for them, her expression shuttered. She
shrugged. "It's okay. They're fake."

Fake? Why would she be wearing fake glasses? He
felt himself gaping at her. She was an odd woman, he
realized. Eccentric. The fuzzy leopard pants had spo-
ken volumes. The granny-style cloak harkened back to
another era. The fake glasses were just another piece
of the puzzle.

Declan sniffed the air around him.

"I'd love to hear all about it, but we really need to
move. Quickly! I smell smoke." He tugged insistently
at her wrist and pulled her to a standing position.

"My purse!" she cried out, reaching down and
yanking it up from the floor.

He fought back against a rising tide of impatience.
Her purse was a luxury at this critical juncture. It certainly wasn't worth either of their lives. "Let's get a
move on," he said as he took Miss Murray by the hand
and led her toward the exit. He let go of her hand as
he worked to disengage the door lock, praying that it
hadn't gotten jammed during the crash landing. If so,
things might get dicey before he could find another
way out of the plane. He uttered a sigh of relief as the
door opened up and he caught a glimpse of the great
outdoors.

Declan raised his hand to protect himself from the
harsh glare of the midday sun. The brightness of the
snow made him blink rapidly a few times. He jumped
out of the plane, then turned around to help his passenger down. He reached for either side of her waist and
lifted her down to the ground. Suddenly she wrapped

her arms around his neck as if her life depended on it. He sputtered as her grip on him tightened. Declan hadn't expected her to treat him like her personal life preserver.

"I think you can let go of me now," he said in a strangled voice. She was gripping him so fiercely, she was cutting off his air supply. Although she was as light as a feather, her choke hold on his neck made it hard for him to breathe.

"I'm so sorry. I think it was all the adrenaline rushing through me," she said as she released her grip on his neck. He set her down on the snow-covered ground. She looked up at him with big brown eyes that were full of apology.

Declan cast a quick glance around him. They had landed smack dab in the middle of the Chugach National Forest. It was a vast area comprised of almost seven million acres of land. His heart lurched painfully inside his chest. Being in a plane crash was bad enough. But surviving in a no-man's-land without food or supplies was another story altogether.

He wasn't a man prone to panic, but if there was ever a moment to give in to that state of being, it was now. They were going to have to do something drastic to help themselves get rescued in this vast, thickly forested area. Although he was putting on a brave front with Annie, he couldn't help but feel that locating them might be akin to finding a needle in a haystack.

So far, Annie's grand adventure had been one big bust. As stressful as her delayed flight had been, it was nothing compared to being a passenger in a plane that had dropped out of the sky and crash-landed in the Alaskan wilderness. Everything had happened so quickly, as if in fast motion. She'd barely had any time to react. Shock had settled in the moment the pilot had announced the upcoming crash landing. All she had been able to do was pray. And wish she had never left the coziness of Maine.

In the moments after the plane touched down, the pilot had helped her out of her seat and toward safety, and although his manner had been a tad gruff, he'd mobilized with an urgency she respected. Clearly time had been of the essence.

As Annie exited the plane, a cold blast of November air hit her squarely in the face. Her eyes teared up. She shivered and drew her cloak tighter around her throat. It was much colder here than back in Maine. She stumbled as her booted feet slid on the snow. Before she could fall on her face, she managed to steady herself.

"Easy there," he warned from behind her. "Watch your step."

"I'm fine," she said. "Just getting my bearings." She looked around her as a feeling of dread coursed through her. They had crashed in the Alaskan wilderness. They were in the middle of a forested area on the last frontier. Otherwise known as the middle of nowhere. Common sense told her that rescue might not come right away. How in the world were they going to manage to make it through this? It was already freezing outside, and they had neither shelter nor a fire to keep themselves warm.

She felt her arm being tugged again. "Miss Murray. We need to stay a safe distance from the plane because it might explode. The inside is on fire."

Explode? Her heart began to thunder in her chest as

the threat of danger hung in the air. A burning scent singed her nostrils. Mr. O'Rourke didn't seem the type who would be prone to exaggeration. He was a pilot, after all. Full of knowledge and wisdom and skill. She felt helpless as he pulled her away from the plane.

Suddenly she stopped in her tracks. "Wait! My bags are still inside. Everything of sentimental value I have in the world is in there!" she cried out.

"Things can be replaced. Our lives cannot," he said in a stern voice that brooked no argument.

He was wrong! Gram's diary was inside her suitcase, along with a blanket Gram had knitted for her as a sixteenth birthday present. Her most cherished keepsake—a picture of her mother cradling her in her arms as a newborn—was also in her luggage. If she lost these precious items, it would be like she'd been severed from her upbringing. She had already lost so much. This would be unbearable.

"No!" she screamed as she lunged toward the plane. For most of her life, she had sat on the sidelines without uttering a peep. She would never forgive herself if she didn't take action in this moment.

Strong arms gripped her shoulders. "What do you think you're doing? Are you trying to get yourself killed?"

Annie felt the hot splash of tears on her cheeks. "I can't stand by and watch it all go up in smoke. My whole life is in there!" She let out a plaintive howl. She saw his ice-blue eyes widen. A muscle in his jaw began to twitch. A low growl escaped his lips. He released her shoulders and pivoted around so that he was facing the plane.

Turning back toward her, he yelled out, "Get out

of this area as fast as you can. Run as far as you can upwind. Now!" She watched as he rushed toward the plane, wrenched open the cargo hold and yanked her suitcases out in one fluid motion. With an amazing display of agility, he ran back toward her at breakneck speed. One look at his expression and Annie began to run in the opposite direction as fast as she could.

A thunderous noise interrupted the silence, followed by a crackling sound rending the air. Unable to stop herself, she turned around and glanced back at the plane. The sight of the fireball caused her knees to buckle. She sank to the ground, giving way to fear and anxiety and shock. If they had lingered a few minutes longer inside the plane, they might not have made it out alive. And because of her, the pilot had almost been blown to smithereens. For all she knew, he could have been injured.

Dear Lord, protect Mr. O'Rourke from harm. I didn't mean to put him in danger. I just didn't want my mementos to be destroyed. Under the circumstances, that might have been selfish. I promise to do better in the future.

She couldn't look away as titian flames licked at the sides of the plane. An acrid odor filled the air. Within seconds, most of the plane had been consumed by the relentless blaze.

Chapter Two

Declan stopped moving in the direction of safety shortly after he heard the massive boom and Lucy went up in a blaze. He stood at a safe distance and stared at his plane as orange flames turned her into a blackened shell of her former self. Pain scorched through him. Lucy was a complete and utter loss! His client's words rang in his ears. *My whole life is in there.* It rang true for him as well. His whole life was O'Rourke Charters, and the planes he owned were essential to the operation of his company. Losing one of his two planes was catastrophic. Although he was thankful that his life and that of his passenger had been spared, there was no escaping the grim reality of his current situation.

He shoved his hand through his hair and muttered angrily. This wasn't fair! With the town of Love having suffered a recession in recent years, his company had already taken some hard financial hits. Because money had been tight and he had never had a single accident, he had opted to lower his insurance premiums. In light of the accident and his destroyed plane, the ramifications were mind-boggling. With limited insurance and a lowered payout for the accident, he had no idea how he would be able to replace Lucy. And without a replacement for his beloved seaplane, he wouldn't be able to run O'Rourke Charters and make a decent living. Not with just one plane left. Everything would be in shambles.

The very thought of it was unfathomable! Who was Declan O'Rourke without his company? *Nobody. Nothing. The son of a convict.* A tiny voice buzzed in his ears. Flying planes was the only thing he'd ever been good at. It was the only vocation he'd ever known.

"Mr. O'Rourke. Are you all right?" The feminine voice splashed over him like a bucket of ice-cold water. It was jarring to be intruded upon at a moment like this. He felt her tugging on his sleeve with an insistence that grated on his nerves.

"Just dandy," he said through gritted teeth. He had almost forgotten about his client. His focus had been wholly consumed by Lucy's destruction. Miss Murray had come up beside him without him even realizing it.

"I called your name three times. You didn't seem to hear me."

He swung his gaze toward her as a numb feeling swept over him. "I didn't," he said in a curt tone. He jutted his chin in the direction of the charred, still-smoking seaplane. "I was a little preoccupied with my life going up in flames."

A little squeak slipped past her lips, and she raised her hand to her throat. "Oh no! Your plane is gone. I'm so sorry. I can't imagine how awful you feel about it." He looked away from her, startled by the raw emotion emanating from her warm brown eyes. She barely knew him, but here she stood, full of concern and sympathy.

Something about her reaction served as a domino effect. The sting of tears blurred his eyes, and he sniffed them away. He never cried. Tears were a sign of weakness. He had learned that lesson as a child at his grandfather's knee. Stiff upper lip. Never let them see you cry. Declan O'Rourke wasn't a weak man. Not by a long shot!

As he always did, he would use humor to diffuse the tension. He was a master at stuffing things down that he didn't want the world to see. He'd been doing it ever since he was a kid. It had always served him well.

"This too shall pass," he murmured, knowing he had been through worse losses in his thirty years. "Honestly, I'm more concerned about my aviator sunglasses. I spent a lot of money on those," he cracked. "Wish I had grabbed them before we exited the plane."

Silence greeted him. Miss Murray's expression was dubious. She raised an eyebrow and twisted her mouth. If he had to guess, he'd say she didn't buy his act.

"If you say so," she said. She held up her cell phone. "There's no cell service. Is there a way to radio for help?"

"We're going to have to wait for rescue. The only radio went up in flames with the plane. I have my cell phone, also, but it's pretty useless without a signal." He shook his head as all the possible avenues for communication with the outside world seemed to evaporate. "I can't imagine they would be able to ping our location in this forest. This area is too remote. When we don't make it back to Love by nightfall, a red flag will be raised. A search and rescue will be put into motion." His chest tightened at the thought of his best friend, Boone Prescott, and his entire family worrying about his demise. Even his brother, Finn, would be put through the ringer by the news, he imagined. Finn, who never took anything seriously, would be forced to face the grim news head-on. "At least for a little bit, there wouldn't be an escape route from the pain and fear and loss, Miss Murray."

"Annie. My name is Annie," she corrected him. "And considering the circumstances we find ourselves in, I think we can use first names when addressing each other."

Declan nodded. "Annie it is. Feel free to call me Declan."

"So, Declan, do you have any idea how long we'll have to wait for rescue?"

He scratched his jaw. "I imagine until morning. By the time the alarm is rung by the FAA and my friends in town, it will be nightfall. They don't routinely send out planes at night to look for crash sites."

"And you registered your flight plan?" she asked, her expression somber.

Her question made him want to grin. Annie Murray knew a little something about planes, he surmised. "Yes, I did, which means they'll be scouring the route we took. Are you an aviation buff?"

"Not exactly. I'm a town librarian. Reading is my superpower," she said with a smile.

Annie's smile packed quite a punch. It reached all the way into his chest cavity and tugged with a mighty force. He shook off the feelings her smile elicited. Annie wasn't his type. The sort of women who appealed to him were classic beauties—tall, elegant, refined. Annie had small town written all over her. Not that there was anything wrong with small towns, but as the product of one, he knew he needed something different in a romantic relationship. Perhaps that was why he hadn't been tempted by any of the women who had arrived in Love to participate in the town's matchmaking enterprise. Although a few of them had made their interest in him known all over town, he hadn't reciprocated their feelings. It was just as well, he realized. The women who had moved to Love were interested in settling down and finding husbands. Declan wasn't the marrying kind, and it would have been cruel to make any woman believe otherwise.

"Well, flying planes is my superpower," he said. He twisted his mouth. Doubt crept in. "Or at least, it was until today."

He scratched his jaw as his mind wandered to the events leading up to the plane's malfunctioning. What had happened? He wasn't entirely sure, which shook him. Everything had happened so quickly. All his attention had been focused on landing the plane safely and ensuring that he and Annie walked away from the plane in one piece. He didn't like all the unanswered questions that were bouncing around in his mind. Had the crash somehow been his fault?

"That's a wonderful superpower to have," Annie said. "I'm very grateful that you were my pilot today. What you did…safely landing the plane…it's rather incredible."

Incredible? He wasn't sure he agreed with Annie, although he appreciated the sentiment. As an experienced pilot, it was his job to avert disaster and to skill-fully maneuver all aspects of aviation.

In his opinion, a crash landing should never have been necessary in the first place. It bothered him deeply that something had gone so catastrophically wrong on his watch.

"Thanks for saying so. I wish that I could have kept us up there in the wild blue yonder. If all had gone well, we'd be getting ready to make our final descent into Love right about now." He shook his head rue-fully. As soon as they made it back to Love, he would begin putting the pieces together in an effort to find out what had gone so terribly wrong with Lucy. He wouldn't rest until he had those answers!

Annie began to shiver right before his eyes. She folded her arms across her chest and rubbed her arms over her cloak in an effort to get warm. He wished he had a blanket to throw over her shoulders. He'd been so preoccupied with their location and the events lead-ing up to the crash that he had allowed his mind to wander from the pressing matters at hand.

"We need to find shelter and hunker down for the night before it gets dark." And he needed to build a fire before they froze to death out here. The fire from the plane had petered out, no doubt due to the snow and ice on the ground as well as the low fuel supply. There had been only enough fuel in Lucy to get them back to Love, which might have been a blessing. If conditions had been different, the blaze from the plane could have spread to the forest and led to a wildfire.

Hmm. He hadn't built a fire since he was a kid on a school wilderness field trip. And even then, Boone had

actually been the one to get it going. He let out a sigh.
Boone had been stepping in to rescue him ever since.

"If you're cold, you should pull something from
your luggage and add another layer," he suggested.
"It may take a bit to get a fire going."

Annie nodded and dug around in her bag until she
produced a knitted blanket. She wrapped it around her
shoulders and let out a contented sigh.

"Where exactly are we?" she asked, looking around
her surroundings with big eyes.

"Midway between Anchorage and Love. We're in
the Chugach National Forest. I spotted it as we flew
overhead. Although this area is sparsely populated
and heavily forested, I seem to recall a campground
in these parts."

He reached into his shirt pocket and pulled out his
trusty compass. It was his habit to carry it around with
him. It was the only earthly keepsake his grandfather
had been attached to during his lifetime. When he had
passed away, Killian O'Rourke had made sure to hand
it off to his favorite grandson. Declan had kept it in
his shirt pocket close to his heart ever since.

And under different circumstances, he might have
been able to use the compass to lead them toward rescue. But there was no way they could navigate their
way out of the forest. And the likelihood of stumbling
across the campground was remote. Surviving in the
wilderness meant making smart choices. He owed it
to both of them to make wise moves from this point
forward.

Now that the shock of the plane crash was beginning to wear off, he had a better viewpoint on their
situation. It was a blessing they had been traveling

over land at the time of the plane trouble rather than Kachemak Bay, where he would have been forced to crash-land on the water. They would have been in the middle of nowhere out on the water with no means of rescue or saving themselves. Hypothermia would have set in shortly. In all likelihood, they would have perished.

Declan began scouting out their immediate area. Knowing it wasn't wise to stray too far from the crash site, he began surveying for the driest area that was protected from the elements. By tonight it would be much colder, with a fierce wind to accompany the temperature drop. There was a copse of pine trees about one hundred feet from the wreckage. Declan walked over to check it out. When he reached the pine trees, he bent down and noticed that there was a relatively dry area between the trees where Annie might be able to make a pallet for sleep. He would stay up tonight to watch out for any signs of rescue or predators. Although it was unlikely that planes would be searching at night, he didn't want to miss any window for rescue.

There was no need to scare Annie by telling her about bears or wolves that roamed the Alaskan wilderness. The last thing he needed was for her to panic. As it was, he was slightly amazed she'd been holding it together. He hadn't pegged her for the calm, cool and collected type.

He walked back over to Annie. She was sitting on a rock and rummaging through her bags with a determined expression plastered on her face. She let out a cry of glee as she pulled out a pair of thick red mittens. "Score! I found them. These will be a game changer. My fingers are frozen."

He nodded approvingly. "Those will definitely help, especially as the temperature drops in a few hours."

She looked up at him with her brows knitted together. "Where are yours?"

Declan shrugged. "I didn't bring any. This was supposed to be only a short flight from Love to Anchorage and then back home." He grinned at her. "I'm not in the habit of bringing mittens on my flights."

She ducked her head and dug back into her bag. A look of triumph flitted across her face as she held up a pair of black mittens with a pink heart on each. "Ta-da! I found another pair. You're welcome to borrow them."

Declan frowned. He wasn't exactly the type of guy who sported mittens with hearts on them. They were super girly. But his hands were getting cold. Annie was holding out the mittens to him with an expectant look on her face. Suddenly he didn't want her to feel bad about his refusing her sweet little mittens. There was something about Annie Murray—eccentricities and all—that reeked of pure goodness.

He reached out and took the mittens from her. "Thanks," he said as he slid them on, letting out a contented sigh as his hands began to warm up from the cold. "You might have just saved my fingers from frostbite."

"Just returning the favor," she said with a huge grin. "After all, you saved both of us with your skilled crash landing. Something tells me not every pilot could have pulled that off." She held out her hands toward the forest. "With all these trees, you had to be dead-on with that landing."

"It's a first for me, Annie. I've never had to make

an emergency landing like this, but I'm thankful for years of flying experience. I learned to fly a plane when most kids are dreaming of getting their first kiss." Declan felt a rush of joy rising up inside him at the memory of his first flying lesson with his grandfather. If he lived to be a hundred, he would never forget the thrill of soaring up above the clouds into the clear blue skies of Alaska. He had felt invincible up in the air, as if none of the heartache and pain of his early years could touch him. And the praise his grandfather had heaped on him had truly made him feel a sense of accomplishment, one he'd never experienced before in his life. For the first time, he'd felt as if he was good at something.

And he was a good pilot. A great one, according to most of his clients. How he wished his grandfather could have seen it all come to fruition. He'd passed away before Declan had gotten his pilot's license. Now O'Rourke Charters had gotten off the ground. The old man would have been so proud and tickled that Declan had made a business out of flying planes, the thing his grandfather had always loved most of all. It hadn't been fair to lose his grandfather to the ravages of diabetes before he'd had the opportunity to give the old man a glimpse of his aviation enterprise. But the one thing life had taught him was that fair hardly ever entered into the equation.

He shook his head in an effort to drag himself out of the past. Those memories could do nothing but hurt him. At the moment, he needed to focus on survival and making it through this ordeal. Night was quickly approaching, and being able to get a fire going would be a huge advantage for them.

He pointed at the area he had just checked out. "That spot over there is probably the best shelter we're going to find. It'll give us a little protection from the elements, and if we can get a fire going, we'll be able to stay warm through the night."

Annie rubbed her hands together. "A fire sounds good. It will save us from hypothermia. I'm sure you're aware of it, but hypothermia sets in when your body core temperature is below ninety-five degrees Fahrenheit. Signs of hypothermia can be drowsiness, confusion, shivering and a slowed-down heart rate."

He nodded his head. As a native Alaskan, he had known about hypothermia before he'd learned to tie his shoes. "Good to know, Annie. I for one do not intend to find that out firsthand," Declan said. "I'm going to make haste and look for some tinder to get the fire going."

Declan began to root around in the brush. He picked up pine needles, shredded bark and a few twigs. When he returned to the makeshift shelter with an armful of tinder, he deposited it in a heap on the ground. He noticed that Annie had moved her belongings over to the site. She had made a little pile of things in front of her seat on a log. With a cheeky grin on her face, Annie held up a granola bar.

"Voilà! It's not a five-course meal, but it should tide us over until tomorrow." She pointed at the pile of snacks set out in front of her.

Declan's stomach grumbled with appreciation at the sight of chocolate, trail mix, beef jerky, peanut butter and crackers. And a bottle of water. For someone who hadn't eaten since this morning, it was a veritable feast. God was good!

"It's a divine meal as far as I'm concerned," Declan said as he accepted the granola bar she held out to him. "It was brilliant of you to bring all these snacks on the flight."

A smile lit up her face. "Not brilliant. Just practical. I sometimes get low blood sugar, so I always make sure I have a bunch of snacks on hand to give me a boost in case I need it. And some of these I stuffed in my luggage. I wasn't sure if peanut butter was big in Alaska. Call me a snack hoarder," she said with a laugh.

"Snack hoard all you want. It's a lifesaver," Declan said, taking a huge bite of a granola bar. He closed his eyes as the morsel slid down his throat. A granola bar had never tasted so good in his life! As hungry as he was, it almost tasted like steak and potatoes.

Annie Murray was shaping up to be quite a woman. She was smart and resourceful and plucky. Right about now he'd expected her to be a sobbing, frightened mess. He really needed to stop making rash and unfair judgments about people. Just because she was wearing fuzzy leopard pants didn't mean she was an airhead. On the contrary, Love's newest transplant was shaping up to be a keeper. Her stash of rations was going to save them from hunger pangs. Thanks to Annie, one of their major problems was solved. Now it was up to him to tackle another issue. Fire.

"As soon as I get this fire going, we'll really be in good shape," he said. This was his moment to demonstrate his skills and to show Annie that he could take charge of the situation and protect her. He took a few dry sticks and began to rub them together frantically. Over and over again he rubbed the sticks in an effort to make a fire out of friction. As soon as he saw a hint of smoke, he would toss the sticks onto the pile of tinder and pray that a roaring fire would start burning.

"How's it going?" Annie asked over his shoulder. She was so close he could feel her breath on his neck. Talk about pressure!

"Any minute now, this tinder is going to go up," he said. "And we are going to have the world's most roaring fire to keep us warm."

Precious seconds ticked by. Frustration began to set in as his efforts to get a fire going failed over and over again. It didn't make any sense at all. Why wasn't this fire sparking? The sticks were dry. He was exerting a lot of energy making sure that there was plenty of friction between the two sticks as he rubbed them together. Yet nothing was happening.

"May I try something?" Annie asked. Declan looked up at her. She was standing beside him and digging around in her purse. What was it with ladies and their purses? The bags almost seemed like an appendage. Annie's purse was like a clown car. She appeared to be able to fit endless items inside.

Bless her for wanting to help with the fire. "This is pretty complicated," he said with a shake of his head. "Have you ever tried to light a fire before?"

He frowned as he watched Annie remove the battery from her cell phone. She then pulled a pocket knife from her bag. "Oh, I've never done it before. But I've read up on the subject. One of the best perks of being a librarian is all the books at our disposal. I find it amazing that knowledge is always at our fingertips."

Declan wanted to groan with frustration. Life wasn't learned through books. Knowledge was accumulated by living. At least, that's the way he'd always handled things. Tackling situations head-on was life affirming and empowering. Burying your head in a book was a surefire way of missing out on life. He didn't want to insult Annie, but he needed to set her straight.

"That's impressive, but starting a fire isn't really something a person can learn from how-to books. Experience is the best way to gain wilderness skills." There was something incongruous about seeing Annie with a pocket knife. "You really did come prepared. Although you really should be careful with that knife. You can hurt yourself if you're not careful."

"In preparation for this voyage, I read a very interesting book about Alaska. It's called *How to Survive and Thrive in the Alaskan Wilderness*. Fascinating stuff," she explained with an enthusiastic nod of her head. "And the first chapter detailed how to start a fire with your cell phone battery."

Declan resisted the impulse to roll his eyes. Thousands of books had been written about the Alaskan wilderness by so-called experts in the field. Not one of them, he would guess, had ever lived in Alaska or knew the first thing about surviving a plane crash. Not a single one would know how to land a malfunctioning seaplane safely. Yet they peddled books about survival to the public.

Annie crouched down next to him and placed the battery on the rock's surface. She scraped the knife against the top of the battery. Then she poked the battery with the knife.

She looked up and met his gaze. "When the lithium is exposed to oxygen, it ignites."

Huh? Book or not, it was pretty impressive. He wasn't sure the everyday, run-of-the-mill librarian knew how to start a fire with a cell phone battery. Annie was a librarian extraordinaire. He swung his gaze toward the battery, which was now smoking. Annie quickly tossed the battery into the tinder pile. Within seconds, smoke began to plume from the tinder. Declan's jaw dropped as he watched a fire burst to life right before their eyes.

"Well, shut my mouth," Declan drawled. "You did it!"

"I did, didn't I?" Annie asked. She was smiling so hard, he thought her cheeks might break. "I feel so invigorated."

He looked down at his twigs and threw them into the fire. "So much for the old-fashioned way," he grumbled. It burned a little to know that Annie had been able to do what he had failed at. Ever since he was a kid, he had hated to have egg on his face. It didn't feel any better as an adult.

Declan felt completely off-kilter. He considered himself an outdoorsman. He fished, mountain climbed and could live off the land if the need arose. Annie was a sheltered librarian from Maine. Up until today, she'd never stepped foot in Alaska. Yet here she was building fires and serving the role of provider with her stash of snacks. Their roles had been flipped. He was the native Alaskan. It was his job as owner of O'Rourke Charters to care for his client, not the other way around.

"Don't feel bad about not being able to start the fire," Annie said in a chirpy voice. "I wouldn't have been able to do it without the battery. And you gathered up all the tinder and made it possible."

Annie was being kind. Her sweet nature radiated off her in waves. He shrugged off his wounded pride and allowed gratitude to wash over him. He was fortunate to have a smart, resourceful woman by his side during this crisis. Survival wasn't a contest. It was a collaborative effort. So far, they had made it through a crash landing, gathered food and water for sustenance and built a fire for warmth. Making sure a rescue plane could spot them from the air was the next important step in their survival plan. It could make the difference between life and death.

He needed to kick things into high gear. His mind had suddenly shifted toward rescue. He needed to do everything possible to make sure that they were rescued tomorrow. At almost eleven thousand square miles, the Chugach National Forest was too large for them to attempt to find rescue on foot. Their food supply wouldn't last much longer, and he was worried about the elements and being able to sustain a fire. If the search and rescue missed the plane wreckage from above, he and Annie Murray would be fighting for their very lives.

Chapter Three

As nightfall came, Annie found herself questioning whether rescue would actually come tomorrow. Her euphoria about starting the fire had waned pretty quickly as the temperature dropped and the sky darkened. What would happen to them if rescue never came? How long could they hold on with a dwindling food supply and no promise of water? At least they could melt snow and drink it, Annie realized. They wouldn't get dehydrated. But there weren't even berries or nuts or anything remotely edible in their midst. And although she wasn't opposed to losing a few pounds, she certainly didn't want to do it via the Alaskan wilderness diet.

She was pretty sure there were wild animals lurking in these woods. Earlier she had heard a high-pitched cry emanating from somewhere in the forest. It had nearly scared the life out of her. Declan had acted nonchalant, as if he hadn't heard a thing. But she knew what she'd heard. Most likely it had been a wolf. Bears tended to hibernate during winter, but there were always sightings during November, especially if the winter weather was mild. So there could be bears waiting to pounce on them. Or wild moose.

She didn't voice her concerns to Declan. His mood had changed in the past hour or so. He seemed more contemplative and less talkative. Perhaps he, too, was worrying about rescue. Maybe he was just the strong, silent type. He certainly looked the part with his muscles and powerful physique. A few times she had caught him staring at her with a perplexed expression on his face. *It wouldn't be the first time*, she thought with a sigh. Men always seemed to think she was quirky.

You're not unusual, pumpkin. You're extraordinary. Again, Gram's voice came to her like a warm breeze over the ocean. As always, pearls of wisdom from Gram fortified her as nothing else ever could.

Eating beef jerky and trail mix, Annie and Declan shared a meal before the fire. Although they had already polished off the sixteen-ounce bottle of water, Annie had filled it back up with snow so that they would have a fresh supply of water when it melted.

The food tasted delicious, although Annie carefully eyed their portions. If rescue didn't come tomorrow, they needed to have a little something to fall back on for a meal. Perhaps it was time to start rationing the food. Declan was a big guy who was probably used to eating big meals.

"So, what brings you to Love?" Declan jutted his chin in her direction. "These days that might seem like an obvious question, considering all the match-making going on."

"Operation Love is what inspired me to come to Alaska. It's been all over the news. I've been very impressed by the coverage." She felt a little self-conscious admitting it, but she wanted to find the love of her life. "I'm no different than most people. I want to find my other half. My soul mate. My husband."

A hint of a smile played around his lips. "Well, so far the program has been a rousing success. My best friend happens to be the town sheriff, as well as the mayor's grandson, and he met the love of his life through Jasper's program."

"Jasper? Mayor Jasper Prescott?" Annie's heart started thumping like crazy. For a good portion of her life, that name had been a constant. Jasper had always featured prominently in Gram's poignant stories about Love. After Gram's death, her journal had revealed tender musings about the handsome charmer who had seemingly captured her grandmother's heart. Her words about Mayor Prescott had made it crystal clear that she had been head over heels in love with him. Perhaps even until her dying day.

And finally, after all these years, Annie was within reach of unraveling the mystery of her ancestry. She was within reach of uncovering her roots. She hoped that would mean family connections. A grandfather. Cousins. Aunts. It was too soon to share her suspicions with Declan, but in her mind, there was a very real possibility that Jasper Prescott was her grandfather. The same Jasper Prescott who had spearheaded the Operation Love campaign and, via the media, urged single women to relocate to his hometown in order to help sort out the woman shortage.

"You'll love Jasper," Declan said. "He's the heart and soul of Love. Town mayor. Wise sage. Loving grandpa. Feisty agitator." He let out a deep-throated chuckle. "He's the man."

Annie knew gushing when she heard it. The respect and admiration Declan felt for Jasper Prescott hummed and vibrated in the air around them. Although Declan didn't radiate a sweet vibe, he suddenly seemed softer and gentler. Clearly the town mayor brought it out in him.

She was going to reserve judgment about Jasper until she knew whether or not he was kin to her. There was a part of her that resented the man who had used his good looks and charm to worm his way into Gram's heart, only to leave her pregnant and alone. The ripples of that situation had affected her own life, since her mother had also been an unwed mother. Annie was determined not to follow the same path. She would break the cycle of women in her family who had loved unwisely and been left to rear children alone.

"It sounds as if you know the mayor well." She touched her forehead with her palm. "Oh, yes, you said that his grandson is a good friend of yours."

"Boone is my best friend. Bar none," Declan asserted with a nod of his head. His blue eyes radiated deep affection. "He's my partner in crime. The one who knows where all the bodies are buried. One of the few people in this world I trust implicitly."

She sensed something under the surface of Declan's words. It was more what he wasn't saying. Who hadn't he been able to trust in his life? Had someone betrayed him? And if so, was that the reason he had a huge chip on his shoulder?

"Will your wife worry about you not making it home?" Although her question wasn't very subtle, she was curious about Declan's life. All she knew about him was that he was an Alaskan pilot. Although she hadn't spotted a ring on his finger, for all she knew, he was married with kids.

"Nope. She won't worry one bit, considering I don't have one," Declan teased, his blue eyes alive with merriment. "I'm single. Footloose and fancy-free. And I aim to keep it that way."

Annie chuckled. She liked the lighter side of Declan, the one who teased and laughed and showed tenderness. She found it rather shocking that someone as eye-catching and successful as Declan was unattached, although from the sound of it, he embraced being a bachelor. If Declan was an example of the eye candy in Love, it was no wonder that women were flocking to the small fishing village to find their soul mates.

"But having grown up in Love, I know plenty of people who will worry when I don't show up." He looked over at her, and their gazes held and locked. His expression was intense. "Don't you worry, Annie. They'll come looking for us."

"I wonder if anybody is waiting for me," she said in a forlorn tone. "I'm the new librarian in Love, so maybe they'll be concerned when I don't arrive on time."

Declan's eyes bulged. He let out a whistle. "So you're *that* librarian."

Annie immediately bristled. She knew bias against librarians when she came up against it. Just when she'd been warming up to Declan, he had to go and say something to put her on edge. "What do you mean by *that* librarian?"

Declan quirked his mouth. "No offense, but resources are tight in town. Taking money out of the town coffers to create a library was a hotly contested topic in Love. We debated it for quite some time."

Annie sat up straight. "I'm working through a partial grant, so all the money isn't coming from the town." She sniffed back tears. She had been so excited about this new adventure. The very thought of being at the center of controversy made her feel terrible. All this time, she had imagined being treated with kindness and support the moment she stepped off the plane. Had she been completely misguided? Maybe she would be as unwelcome as a storm sweeping into town.

"Hey, now," Declan said, his voice noticeably softer. He edged closer her and peered into her face. "Are you…crying?"

"No, I'm not," she said as tears splashed onto her cheeks. "It's just smoke from the fire getting in my eyes." She was mortified. Up to this point, she had managed to hang tough and hold her head up high. All of sudden she had broken like a dam.

He reached out and brushed her tears away with his thumb. "Forgive me. I spoke without thinking, Annie. It's been a really long, scary day for you. All you expected when this day began was to arrive safely in Love, Alaska, with a wonderful adventure stretched out before you. And what did you get instead? A terrifying crash landing in the middle of the wilderness. And a pilot who has a bad habit of putting his foot in his mouth."

Annie stared into Declan's eyes, lulled by the rich timbre of his voice and his ice-blue eyes. He really was a spectacular-looking man. And he was kind. He just hid it behind a mask of brusqueness. He'd been hurt, she deduced. Someone or something had bruised this man, and as a result, he hid his light under a bushel. But without him even knowing it, the richness of his soul shone through at certain moments.

"I'm sorry for being so thoughtless with my words. I really like you, Annie Murray. You have more spirit and pluck than most women would have in a crisis like this. And you've done brilliantly in an unpredictable and terrifying situation. Truth be told, I'm pretty fortunate that you were my passenger. Without you here, I'd be hungry and cold and downright miserable. If I had to rate you as a survival companion, I'd give you an A plus."

Annie smiled at Declan through her tears. He was being so very kind to her. The truth was, he had bruised her feelings with his careless comment about what the town thought of her. She took her profession very seriously, and if she was being completely honest, she was a tad homesick. Whimsy, Maine, was all she had ever known. And she had traveled all this way to head up Love's new library, only to be involved in a plane crash. The last thing she needed to worry about was her bread-and-butter job in Alaska.

But to be fair, it wasn't completely Declan's fault. Her nerves had already been on edge. This day had been endless. And she was scared to death. It was almost time to go to sleep, and she didn't know what the morning would bring. Rescue? Or vast disappointment?

"I don't know if I deserve all your praise, but I appreciate you lifting me up."

Declan flashed her a perfect smile. "Anytime, Annie. We're buddies now, right? After this singular experience, we're bonded for life."

Bonded for life. What a dramatic turn of phrase. Even though she knew better than to fall for a handsome charmer like Declan, the idea of being bonded for life with him was not an unwelcome thought.

When it was time to bunk down for the night, Declan borrowed several articles of clothing from Annie so that he could make a pallet for himself. He intended to keep watch tonight rather than lie down and sleep. He figured if he propped the pallet against a tree, he could sit up and keep watch without being too uncomfortable. And he felt the need to keep watch over Annie. Even though she acted tough, Annie Murray needed protection. Until he delivered her safely to Love, she would be under his watchful, protective eye.

He and Annie enjoyed a companionable silence as they made their pallets. Declan couldn't fathom how she had managed to stuff so many items in her bags.

"I feel bad getting all your clothes dirty," Declan said.

"Oh, don't worry," Annie said with a wave of her hand. "I sent two trunks of clothing ahead of me through a shipping service. After all, a girl can never have too many clothes," she quipped.

Declan gaped at her. More clothes? It was fairly mind-boggling how one woman could own so many outfits. They sat there for a few moments in stillness.

"After what we've been through together, I feel compelled to tell you something I haven't shared with a lot of people." Annie's announcement interrupted the quiet that had stretched out between them.

Declan eyed her nervously. Annie was as sweet as blueberry pie, but he didn't really want to head into the territory of TMI. It might create an uncomfortable vibe between them if she overshared. After all, they didn't really know each other well enough to exchange personal information. He had no intention of spilling any secrets of his own.

"It's about my fake glasses." She let out a sigh. "You're probably wondering why I would do such a thing, right? I never explained myself." Declan nodded as a sense of relief flooded him. A confession about glasses he could handle.

"When I first became a librarian, I was twenty-three years old. I was given the job because the head librarian in my hometown of Whimsy, Rose Minnows, passed away. She was ninety-five, bless her heart."

Declan sputtered. "Your town librarian was ninety-five?"

Annie nodded her head enthusiastically, causing locks of her dark brown hair to cascade over her forehead. "She was two weeks shy of her ninety-sixth birthday when the Lord called her home to glory."

Declan let out a low whistle. "That's dedication to a vocation. Ninety-six!"

Annie nodded solemnly. "Rose was the consummate professional. So when I replaced her, everyone in town questioned whether I was fit for the job due to my age. Of course it was hurtful, considering I had grown up in Whimsy, and the same people who had rocked me on their knees were now questioning my abilities. I decided that I would do everything in my power to convince the townsfolk I was the perfect choice for head librarian. Step one was to switch up my wardrobe. I dressed the part of a town librarian—"

"You mean that you dressed in a dowdy manner?" Declan interrupted.

"Dowdy?" Annie asked with a frown. "Of course not. Rose was the most beautifully dressed woman in town. She put the *F* in fashion, if you know what I mean."

"Not sure I do," he muttered. "Jeans and my aviator jacket are my fashion statement."

"Her clothes were classic. Timeless." Annie let out a sigh. "Step two was to wear glasses. I know it may sound strange, but people are judged all the time by appearances. In our society, glasses signify intelligence. Wisdom. The moment I slipped the glasses on, people began to treat me differently. It was night and day. Suddenly I was fit for duty simply because of my appearance." She brushed some pine needles off her leopard pants. "So that's the story behind my glasses. I figured they might help me out here in Love as well. But I guess I'm on my own in that department." A little sigh slipped past her lips.

"Don't worry about what I said earlier, that the library is a hot-button issue. We debate everything in Love. That's who we are. All the wrinkles about funding for the library will probably be ironed out." *Or not*, Declan thought guiltily. He himself had lobbied to reduce the number of hours the library was being funded. It hadn't been a malicious move on his part. Love's first library had gone belly-up decades ago due to lack of funding. He just couldn't wrap his head around using vital town resources so people could browse for books. Not when there were businesses still suffering in town. However, there was no way in the world he could admit that to Annie. Not at the moment, anyway.

Annie frowned. "Wrinkles? There are wrinkles?"

He let out a groan. There he went again, spilling information he should have kept close to the vest. On the other hand, Annie had traveled a long way to become town librarian in Love. She deserved the unfiltered truth. "There are a few," he said in a halting voice. "Sorry to be the bearer of bad news, but the library has only been approved for part-time hours."

"But that's ridiculous," she exploded. "Mayor Prescott told me weeks ago that the library budget had been approved and that I was being brought on as a full-time librarian."

Declan held up his hands. "Don't shoot the messenger. I just didn't want you to feel blindsided."

Annie bowed her head. "I'm sorry for blowing up at you. Thanks for telling me. I think," she said in a soft voice.

"You're welcome. Why don't you get some sleep, Annie?" he suggested. "It's been a long day."

Annie yawned and stretched her arms. "I am pretty bushed. Good night, Declan." She walked toward her pallet, which was a good distance from his, where he was keeping watch.

"Night," he called out after her. "Don't get too close to the fire. We don't want any accidents."

He watched from afar as Annie settled down on her pallet. She was close enough to the fire that she could feel warm and toasty without endangering herself. She had said earlier that her boots were doing a pretty good job of keeping her feet warm, although at the very tip, she felt a little spot where her toes were cold. Once they got to Love, he was going to buy her a pair of Hazel Tookes's boots. Hazel was a good friend of his who had created unique Alaskan winter boots that the town of Love was now mass-producing. Boone's wife, Grace, had come up with the brilliant idea of making Hazel's boots the focus of the town's moneymaking endeavors. So far, Hazel's boots were selling like hot cakes in the lower forty-eight states. If the income streaming in from the boots continued, it could be a game changer for Love.

An unsettled feeling kept poking at him. He hadn't told Annie the whole unvarnished truth about the library hours being reduced. He had lobbied against the library, and after it had been approved, he had been a proponent of reducing its hours. He couldn't help but feel guilty about Annie's job being slashed by a significant number of hours.

As Declan watched Annie doze off, he felt a surge of protectiveness rise up within him. There was something about her that brought out a desire in him to keep her safe. And he wasn't sure it had anything to do with his duties as a pilot. He vowed that no matter what situation arose, he would keep Annie out of harm's way. He uttered a silent prayer that the morning would bring rescue. If not, he was going to have to come up with a plan B in order to ensure that they made it out of this crisis alive.

Annie was dreaming of Love, Alaska. Ice-skating at Deer Run Lake. Wintry nights. A tight-knit community where she would be welcomed with open arms.

A spanking new library that changed lives, one book at a time. A soft place to fall when the world around her became chaotic. A strapping, tall man with golden hair and a magnetic smile.

She heard a flapping noise by her ear. She raised her hand to brush it away. Something furry was swirling around her neck. Oh no! This wasn't a dream. This was real life. Something was burrowed in her hair. With a scream lodged in her throat, Annie sat up straight and started fighting it off with her fists. She managed to get it out of her hair. By the glow of the fire, she could see wings and squinty little eyes as he began flying around her in circles.

"Bat!" she yelled as the fuzzy brown critter swooped down at her. Once again it burrowed in her hair as she began to jump around wildly in an effort to dislodge it.

She had almost died earlier today in a plane crash. And now she was on the brink of being killed by a rabid bat bent on taking her down. She began shrieking at the top of her lungs.

"Declan! Help!"

It was a perfect Alaskan day. The sun was shining brightly in a robin's-egg-colored sky. Declan soared above the clouds without a care in the world. Everything felt peaceful up here in the wild blue yonder, as if nothing bad could ever touch him again.

Something was wrong. He was flying Lucy. No, that wasn't possible. Hadn't Lucy gone up in flames?

Screams jolted him awake. As soon as Declan heard the word *bat*, his entire body froze up. Bats! The one thing in the world that he didn't want to deal with head-on. Give him bears, wild moose and wolves. He'd take those animals on any day of the week without batting an eye. He had hated bats ever since one had bitten him when he was six years old. He and Boone had been spelunking in Nottingham Woods when they had stumbled upon a group of bats. Declan felt a chill crawl down his back at the memory.

He sat up straight and looked over at Annie. She was on her feet, jumping up and down while yelling at the top of her lungs. Pushing past the terror, he leaped up from his pallet and raced over to Annie's side.

"Bat!" she screamed again, pointing toward her hair. The bat was tangled up in her shoulder-length brown hair.

Declan searched the strands and immediately spotted a flapping bat's wing. Thankful for Annie's extra pair of mittens, he wrenched the bat from Annie's tangled locks and hurled it to the ground. For a moment, the bat sat on the ground, seemingly stunned.

"I hope the poor critter is okay," Annie said in a fretful tone.

With a wild cry, it flapped its wings and took off, soaring into the black night.

Annie stared after the bat as it flew off into the distance. "I was sort of hoping this was all a dream. There really was a bat in my hair, wasn't there?"

"Yes, there was," Declan said, still amazed by the turn of events. What more could this day possibly bring? A snowstorm and a pack of wolves?

"They can be dangerous if they bite you," Annie said.

"Did it bite you?" he asked, alarmed. That was the last thing they needed to take this crisis over the top.

Her lips trembled. "I'm not sure. I don't think so. Can you look for me?"

Declan lifted her hair up and away from her neck. He inspected one side, then the other. There was no evidence of a bat bite. No marks whatsoever. "I don't see anything, Annie. I think you're good."

Her shoulders sagged with relief. "Phew. Bats can carry rabies. Although most don't, it would be unfortunate to be bitten by a rabies-infested bat." She stood on her tiptoes and pressed a kiss against Declan's cheek. "Thank you. That's the second time you saved my life. All in one day. You really are a superhero, Declan O'Rourke."

Superhero. Just hearing her say that word made his chest swell to twice its normal size. His heart began thrumming like a drumbeat.

Declan didn't say a word as Annie settled back onto her pallet. She took her cloak and wrapped it around her face and torso, then burrowed under her clothes. Clearly she wasn't taking any more chances with bats.

He raised his hand to his cheek and let out a ragged sigh. The kiss from Annie had come out of nowhere. Things had suddenly gotten very complicated. His chest tightened, and he swallowed past the emotions rising to the surface. He didn't even want to analyze what he was feeling in this moment. It had been such a long time since he had felt anything simmering between himself and an attractive, appealing woman.

It didn't matter. He couldn't allow anything romantic to develop between them. Annie Murray wasn't his type. She was looking for a husband. He had no intention of courting a small-town librarian who was in search of a soul mate. Although Operation Love was a smashing success in his opinion, he didn't want to be matched up with anyone. He had long ago reached the conclusion that he wasn't the settling-down type.

The past had taught him that happily-ever-afters weren't meant for everyone, especially not the son of Colin O'Rourke.

From what he'd seen, Annie was way too sensitive for his liking. He'd already made her cry. And he didn't like the way she rattled things off as if she was a walking encyclopedia. After a while it might get old to have someone constantly spouting off facts like a know-it-all. It felt awkward that he had opposed library funding. He hadn't had the heart to tell her that. He had been way too unnerved earlier by her tears. And something told him she would have been as mad as a hornet at the discovery.

Considering the fact that the town was still struggling to get back on its feet, funding a library didn't seem practical. It was one thing for the town to support businesses like Hazel's Lovely Boots, but a library wasn't going to bring money to Love. It was simply going to put a strain on an already tight town budget.

All that was fine and good. But the moment Annie's lips had pressed against his cheek, something had shifted a little bit inside him. Something that deeply worried him. She had just stirred up feelings inside him that he hadn't experienced in a very long time. Feelings that terrified him way more than any bat ever could.

Chapter Four

Annie felt as if she had barely put her head down on her pallet before morning came, bringing with it hope for rescue and fear of the unknown. For a few moments, she sat back and enjoyed the sunrise as it crept into being. Oranges, pinks and purples graced the sky, serving as a reminder that God was all around her. He had created this magnificent scenery. And He would see to it that she and Declan made their way to Love. She knew it all the way down to the tips of her toes.

She swept her gaze around her. The fire that had burned so brightly last night was now barely a flame. The warmth it had provided was a thing of the past. Her tingling fingers could attest to that fact. At least it was still burning, which meant it could be resurrected. She raised her arms over her head and stretched, casting a quick glance in the direction of Declan's pallet. He was still propped against the tree, but his eyes were pressed closed and he was fast asleep.

She felt a surge of gratitude for this strong, sturdy man who had been her anchor during this crisis. He had not only saved their lives by executing a perfect landing in the wilderness but also rescued her from a bat's clutches and saved all her belongings from the plane. Declan had taken care of her, something she hadn't experienced a whole lot in her life. One of the reasons she had always been so independent was that, other than Gram, there had been no one to lean on.

Annie let out a sigh as she stood up and headed toward the fire. If it was going to continue to burn, she was going to have to stoke it. Declan had stayed up through the night to accomplish that task. She was guessing that he had finally fallen asleep due to utter exhaustion.

Even though they were still stranded in the middle of Chugach National Forest and there was no hint of imminent rescue, she still felt blessed. They were alive and uninjured. And according to Declan, a search party would be looking for them today. Hope was ever present.

"Morning." Declan's deep voice startled her. His eyes were now wide open, and he was greeting her with a lazy smile.

"I thought you were asleep," she said, hoping he didn't think she had been staring at him. Gorgeous specimens like Declan were probably used to being drooled over. Not that she had been drooling in any way, shape or form. Simply admiring from afar.

"Just resting my eyes," he said. He stood up and brushed off his pants, then headed toward her. "I'm glad the fire is still going. Now that it's morning, I'm guessing we'll see some planes overhead."

"Do you think we'll see them soon?" she asked eagerly.

He nodded. "Once dawn broke, they probably

began mobilizing. We need to be ready on our end so that we don't waste a precious second."

Annie clapped her hands together. "What's the plan?" She blinked at him. "You do have a plan, don't you?"

He winked at her. "Declan O'Rourke always has a plan." He grinned at her, then walked back over to his pallet and reached down to pull out a square box. He turned back toward her and held it up in the air. "This emergency kit is about to secure our rescue."

Annie furrowed her brow. "What's in there?"

Declan popped the kit open and pulled something out. "A flare," he said in a triumphant voice. "We can only use it once, so we have to wait for the exact moment to set it off. The colored smoke can be seen from quite a distance, so we'll have a good shot of being seen from the air. It will be instantly recognizable as a distress signal."

Annie felt her pulse sizzle with excitement. "Oh, that's an excellent plan. It was quick thinking of you to grab the emergency kit from the plane. How many flares are in there?"

Declan's smile disappeared. "Just this one. When I say this has to go off perfectly without a hitch, I'm not exaggerating. It's possible they might see a fire from above if we get a big one going, but if it gets out of control, this whole forest could go up. I'm not willing to risk that."

"Nor am I," Annie said with a firm nod of her head. "The flare has to work."

A sigh escaped Declan's lips. "Why don't we eat something for breakfast? It could be hours before they scour this area. I'm going to keep the flare inside the kit so it can stay nice and dry. As soon as we hear any planes circling overhead, I can set off the flare."

They settled down on logs beside the reinvigorated fire and indulged in peanut butter and crackers. Annie broke off a square of chocolate for each of them. Not much conversation flowed between them as they ate. Annie's mind was occupied by thoughts of being rescued and what might happen if it didn't come to pass. What would happen to them? According to Declan, the forest was too vast for them to walk toward rescue.

Would they just wither away into nothing or be devoured by a pack of wild Alaskan wolves? Even though she knew her thoughts were dramatic, they didn't seem that far-fetched considering their predicament.

Within minutes, Annie heard a rumbling noise that seemed to emanate from the sky. At first she wasn't certain if she was imagining it or not. Then the sounds became more persistent. Declan jumped up from the log he was sitting on. He looked upward, concentration etched on his face.

"Is that—?" she began. Her heart was pounding like a jackhammer.

"Yes! I'd know that sound anywhere," Declan shouted as he opened the kit and yanked out the flare. He stood up and craned his neck. Annie followed Declan's lead and began scouring the sky for a plane. Suddenly the rumbling sound got louder.

"There!" she shouted, pointing to the sky as she spotted a red-and-white plane flying above them.

Just as the plane flew directly overhead, Declan extended his arm and raised the flare in the air. Feeling as if she could barely breathe, Annie watched as colored smoke filled the sky.

"Turn around," Declan said through gritted teeth. His eyes were focused on the sky. His hands were clenched at his sides.

"Oh no!" Annie fretted. "It's not turning around. They didn't see the smoke."

The plane disappeared from view just as quickly as it had appeared. Annie raised her hands to cover her mouth so she didn't let out a sob of disappointment. She had been hopeful about Declan's plan for them to be rescued. This felt like a devastating blow.

"Just give it a minute," Declan said. He was saying something over and over again under his breath. She couldn't quite make out the words. She felt numb. What would they do now? Even if they screamed at the top of their lungs, no one would ever hear them.

Suddenly the plane came back into view. It began circling above them. Within minutes, it began to descend, bit by bit. It was coming for them!

Declan waved his arms high in the air. "They see us, Annie. They see us!" His face was lit up with joy. Unable to contain herself, Annie jumped up and down. She hooted and hollered. Declan's grin stretched from ear to ear. They were both ecstatic.

"Oh, Declan! We're saved. Isn't it wonderful?"

"It's beyond wonderful," Declan gushed as he swept her up in his arms, then twirled her around. Annie felt almost giddy as her feet left the ground and Declan whirled her in the air. As he settled her back on the snow-covered ground, she looked up at him and directly into his ice-blue eyes. Their gazes held and locked. Something simmered in the air between them that caused her legs to shake like the branches of an unstable tree.

Having never experienced this particular feeling before, all Annie could do was pray. *Dear Lord, please keep my feet firmly planted on earth. Declan is not the right man for me, regardless of the way he makes my heart race. Please allow me to continue the path You have been leading me on. The path straight to Love.*

Declan tried to catch his breath. Between their imminent rescue and the romantic tension brewing between him and Annie, he couldn't decide which was causing his pulse to race more. He stepped back from Annie and swung his gaze toward the sky. He began waving his arms in the air again until the plane dipped down farther and farther. From this vantage point he recognized the plane as his own, Ethel. Within the space of a few minutes, it landed in a clearing about three hundred feet away from them. Declan let out the breath he had been holding since the very moment he knew Lucy was in trouble. He felt as if the weight of the world had suddenly been lifted off his shoulders.

There was only one person who knew how to fly Ethel with such finesse. Finn! He knew that his brother was the pilot as surely as he knew his own name. Boone was the first one to step out of the plane. He made a beeline toward Declan. A few moments later, Finn emerged. He stood next to the plane, shifting his weight from one foot to the other. He hung back and surveyed everything going on around him.

Declan met Boone halfway, thrilled to the bone that his best friend had come looking for him. In truth, he wouldn't have expected any less from him. Their relationship had always been rock solid. Boone clapped him on the shoulder before saying, "Do you have any idea of what you put us through?"

Before he could even respond, Boone wrapped him up in a bear hug. Declan went with it, hugging Boone back with equal ferocity. When the hug ended after a few moments, Declan took a good look at his best friend. Boone appeared as wrecked as Declan felt. Boone's chin trembled. A sheen of moisture gathered in his eyes. He shook his head. "I've never been more relieved to see anyone in my whole life, Declan."

"Thanks for coming to find me," Declan said, feeling overwhelmed with the emotion of the moment. In all the years of their friendship, Boone had never once let him down. He hoped Boone could say the same about him.

"Don't thank me. I just came along for the ride. Finn was the one who organized everything," Boone said, jutting his chin in Finn's direction. "He really came through in the clutch. We were desperate to locate you."

Declan reluctantly swung his gaze in his brother's direction. Finn was standing off to the side with his hands jammed in his back pockets. He was next to Annie, who was talking a mile a minute. Declan studied his brother for a moment. With his dark hair and emerald green eyes, Finn didn't really look like him, although they shared a similar build and height. As far as Declan was concerned, they were polar opposites. Declan needed human contact in his life, while Finn was content to backpack by himself in the Himalayas for weeks at a time. Finn ran away from life, while Declan had always been the one to stick around and face the problems head-on. It had put them at odds for most of their lives.

He had to give it to Finn, though. For once, he'd come through for him.

Annie and Finn made their way over to them. Finn held out his hand so Declan could give him their special knuckle bump. They'd been doing it ever since they were kids.

"Glad you're still in one piece," Finn said, his expression shuttered. But Declan could see the telltale sign of his brother's distress. A bluish vein was jumping around by his eye. It was a nervous tic he had. It spoke volumes about his current stress level.

"It would take more than a plane crash to take me down," Declan said in a teasing voice. Boone shot him a questioning look. His best friend hated when he minimized serious situations and hid his real feelings behind a jovial mask. Later on, when he was safely back in Love, he could let his guard down and fall apart a little. For now, he was going to try his best to hold it together.

"Annie, this is Boone Prescott, otherwise known as the sheriff of Love, Alaska." Declan said. He shot Boone a pointed look. "Boone, this is Annie Murray, our new town librarian."

Annie beamed at Boone and held out her hand. "Nice to meet you, Sheriff. I'm thrilled to make your acquaintance, but I wish it was under less stressful circumstances."

Boone shook Annie's hand and said, "It's a pleasure, Annie. I hope this misadventure doesn't tarnish your opinion about Alaska."

"Not one little bit," Annie said. "How many people

can say they crash-landed in an Alaskan forest and lived to tell the tale?" She let out a chuckle. "I'll be telling this story to my grandkids."

"Annie has been terrific." Declan rushed in to praise her. "First time in Alaska and she handled herself like a pro after the crash. She lit a fire, kept us with food in our bellies and maintained her cool in a harsh and unforgiving environment."

Annie's face turned a pretty pink shade as she waved her hand at him. "Don't listen to him. He puts the *H* in hero, if you know what I mean."

"The two of you are a regular mutual admiration society," Boone drawled, his lips twitching with amusement.

Uh-oh. Declan frowned. He knew that look. Boone made that face whenever he was teasing him about a prospective love interest. Declan needed to set Boone straight in no uncertain terms. Annie was a tender-hearted librarian looking to settle down and live out her dreams. He was the last man in Love who could offer her the white picket fence and promises of forever. Those things were meant for other men. Not him.

Just knowing that he wasn't capable of such a huge commitment caused an uncomfortable pressure to lodge against his chest. More and more these days he was finding himself wishing things could be different. Seeing Boone's whole life open up after meeting Grace served as proof that true love was possible.

When Boone continued to grin at him, Declan subtly jabbed him in the side. He swiftly veered the subject toward another topic. "And it looks like you've already met my brother, Finn," Declan said, nodding in his brother's direction.

"I sure did," Annie gushed. "I'm mighty impressed that both of you are pilots. You must make your parents really proud."

An uncomfortable silence followed Annie's statement. Declan was used to people in his hometown avoiding the topic of his parents at all costs. It was impossible for his mother to be proud of her boys since she had died when he was eight. And he had no clue whether his father felt proud of him or not. Declan hadn't seen his father since he was sentenced to ten years in prison. Truthfully he wasn't sure he even wanted to.

Finn recovered first. "Declan is the real deal," Finn said. "I might have the technical ability, but Declan here has all the heart. That's a powerful combination."

Hearing his brother say those words warmed his insides. It was a rare moment when the two of them lifted each other up. So many things stood between them as a result of their dysfunctional past. He used to pray for a better relationship with Finn. Without even realizing it, he had long ago stopped asking God for help in that area of his life.

"Thanks for the rescue, Finn," Declan said with a nod of his head. "In a few hours, things would have gotten dicey," Declan admitted. Although he didn't want to dwell on what might have happened, it was a reality he couldn't simply ignore.

Finn quirked his mouth. "No problem. That's what big brothers are for," he said with a smirk. "Besides, it gave me an opportunity to fly Ethel."

"Ethel?" Annie asked with a raised eyebrow. "Don't tell me. You named this plane, also."

Finn leaned in. "He sure did. Ethel and Lucy are the great loves of Declan's life."

Boone laughed and threw back his head. "So that explains why he's still single," he said. "I've been racking my brain trying to figure it out."

Declan couldn't resist laughing along with his best friend. It was funny the way things had worked out. Finn had been itching to fly Ethel for the longest time. Declan had a hard-and-fast rule. No one flew his O'Rourke Charter planes but himself and his employee, Willard, since both were listed on the insurance. Today Finn had found a loophole in the policy, and as a result, he'd been given the opportunity to fly Declan's cherished plane.

His brother had learned to fly at the same age as he had, and in his opinion, Finn was just as good a pilot as he was, even though he'd long ago decided he didn't want to fly planes for a living. The plan had always been for him and Finn to open O'Rourke Charters together, until Finn had bailed on him at the last minute. Declan had been forced to scramble to get the funds together to live out his dream. Thanks to Boone and the Prescott family, Declan's dream hadn't gone up in smoke.

Finn's betrayal still stretched out between them like a live electrical wire. *Fool me once, shame on you. Fool me twice, shame on me.*

His older brother had been letting him down for most of their lives. Declan considered himself a fool for ever truly believing that he would come through for him. Finn had always had one eye on the nearest exit out of Love. Declan had given up on the idea of his brother ever putting down roots in their hometown. He'd come back for a few months, then fly off again on his latest adventure. He was a lot like their father in that regard. Finn never wanted to plant roots anywhere.

"She flies like a dream," Finn said with a nod of his head. "I expect you'll be wanting to fly her back."

Fly her back? Fear slithered through Declan at Finn's words. Just the thought of getting into the cockpit again made him break out in a cold sweat. It was such a foreign feeling to him to be nervous about flying, but he couldn't ignore the emotions roaring through him. Terror. Nervousness. Suddenly he was right back in that desperate moment when Lucy had fallen from the sky and he had been in a life-and-death struggle at the controls. Everything had happened so quickly. He'd barely had time to react.

What would have happened if he had made a single misstep? He shuddered. Finn was studying him, a look of curiosity flickering in his eyes.

"Nah," he said with a shake of his head. "Why don't you fly us home, Finn? I didn't get much sleep last night," he said. Finn's eyes widened. Boone gaped at him.

"Seriously?" Finn asked. He let out a loud cackle of delight. "I never would have thought you'd let me fly Ethel home."

Boone eyed him suspiciously. "Are you sure that you didn't hit your head in the crash?"

"I did not hit my head. I'm in perfect health, which is fairly extraordinary, considering we crash-landed in no-man's-land." Declan asserted.

Boone clapped him on the shoulder. "It's time we head home. You need some food and some rest, not to mention some time to process everything that's happened."

"I'm fine," Declan said, knowing as soon as the words left his mouth that it was far from the truth. He wasn't fine. The crash had changed him. Just one glance in Ethel's direction had his heart thundering inside his chest. He prayed this feeling wouldn't last, but for the life of him, he couldn't imagine ever wanting to fly her again.

During the flight to Love, Annie couldn't help but sneak a few glances at Declan. He was seated in the row across from her. Sheriff Prescott was in the row behind them, reclining with his legs stretched out on the seat next to him. Ethel was a bit roomier than Lucy, she realized. She didn't feel quite so claustrophobic on this plane. Or perhaps she was just so happy to have been rescued that she was viewing things with different eyes.

She might have been imagining it, but Declan didn't seem as bold and confident as he had a mere twenty-four hours ago. He was drumming his fingers on his knee and glancing back and forth between the window and the cockpit.

He seemed antsy. Preoccupied. Maybe he was wishing he was flying the plane rather than Finn. Perhaps he couldn't stop thinking about the plane crash. Even though she was slightly nervous about the flight, she hadn't been the one who had been flying the plane. She couldn't imagine all the turmoil Declan must be facing, particularly since his flying record had been spotless prior to yesterday. On impulse, she unbuckled her seat belt and went over to sit beside him.

Declan eyed her with surprise. His thick blond hair was a bit tousled, and he had a sleepy expression on his face as if he might need a good night's rest.

"You looked like you might need a pick-me-up," she said, her eyes skimming his face. His expression was a tad beleaguered, although it did nothing to diminish him in the looks department.

"I'm okay. Just a little weary. I get a little off-kilter when I don't get my full eight hours of sleep," Declan explained.

A hint of sadness hung over him. She recognized it. More than anything, she wanted to make him laugh, to see the spirited side of him that she knew was lurking inside.

"I have a joke for you. What did the pencil say to the other pencil?" she asked.

He tapped his finger against his chin. "Hmm." After a few seconds he shrugged. "I don't know."

"You're looking sharp," Annie said. "Get it? Sharp. Pencil." Annie jabbed him playfully in the side.

Seemingly against his will, the corners of Declan's mouth began to twitch with laughter. He settled back against his seat and chuckled. All of a sudden, his face resembled sunshine and blue skies.

Annie pointed at him. "See, I was able to make you laugh. Mission accomplished."

Declan chuckled and shook his head at her. "That joke was so bad, it was good."

Annie giggled. "Ouch! Well, at least you found it amusing."

Declan reached out and placed his hand over hers. "Thanks, Annie, for being such a peach. I really meant it when I said you were fantastic out there in the forest. You showed a lot of heart and pluck and grit. And I know you were scared. But it didn't stop you from fighting for survival and giving it your best. That's what separates the ordinary from the extraordinary." He squeezed her hand. "For what it's worth, I think you're one in a million."

Annie felt tears pricking her eyes. She blinked them away. Her chest swelled with pride. "That's awfully kind of you to say, Declan."

"I'm not being kind. Just truthful. The town of Love is fortunate to have you as its newest citizen." He was looking at her with such sincerity and goodness that, for a moment, she almost thought she heard a chorus of violins playing. She let out an unintentional sigh, earning herself a questioning look from Declan.

"I'm going to tell you something that I haven't told a single other confidant. A secret." She repositioned herself and edged closer, so that her shoulder was now brushing against his arm.

Declan raised his eyebrow. "What's the secret?"

"You asked me why I was coming to Love." She felt her smile widening into a huge grin. "I only told you half the story." Annie turned toward the back of the plane to make certain the sheriff was still sleeping. After hearing the light buzz of his snoring, Annie turned back to Declan. "I not only intend to find my other half here in Alaska and serve as town librarian but I also plan to find my long-lost family in Love."

Declan's brows knit together. "Your long-lost family, huh? What is this, some genealogy investigation?" He chuckled lightly. "Are you going to be taking DNA samples?"

She wrinkled her brow. Declan seemed to think she

was kidding. "Nothing that scientific, I'm afraid. At least, not right away. After my grandmother passed away last year, I began to read her journals. She was born and raised in Love. I grew up hearing heart-warming tales about life in your quaint little fishing village." Another sigh slipped past her lips. "She made Love sound like something out of a fairy tale. When she left Alaska for Maine all those years ago, she was pregnant with my mother. Gram never revealed the identity of the father, so my mother, bless her heart, never knew who he was."

"That's a shame," Declan said. "Everyone has a right to know who they are." There was something radiating from Declan's voice that made her believe he knew where she was coming from. He empathized with her situation. Relief washed over her. She had made the right decision by confiding in him.

"Exactly!" Annie said, her voice rising with excitement. "Gram's diary pretty much tells the tale of the man she was in love with. A good-looking charmer she grew up with. She worshipped the very ground he walked on. And my goal is to meet this man and prove that he's my grandfather. After all, I really don't have any other family connections."

Declan's mouth twisted. "Annie, I understand your motivations, but don't you think it might be a bit more complicated than some scribblings in a journal? That's not really proof of anything."

"But she left me plenty of bread crumbs. And the names of her best girlfriends and the boys who were in their circle. She left enough clues for me to figure it out." Annie leaned in so that she could speak softly in his ear. She didn't want to run the risk of Boone overhearing her in case he wasn't fully asleep. Getting up close and personal with Declan wasn't half-bad, she realized. He smelled of pine trees and the great outdoors. All of a sudden, she was having trouble concentrating. She had lost her train of thought.

Declan regarded her, a look of puzzlement etched on his face. "It sounds a bit tricky."

"I promise you, it's not complicated at all. Every word she wrote about him shimmers with meaning."

"Does her journal say why she left town? Was it because she was pregnant?" Declan asked. His brows were knitted together.

Annie shook her head. It was something she'd always wondered about, especially since Gram had avoided the topic. "No, it doesn't. Matter of fact, the journal ends rather abruptly. Right around the time she left Alaska for Maine."

"Do you think perhaps she didn't want anyone to know? It sounds like she had ample time to tell you if she'd wanted to share that information."

"Gram was always ashamed of being a single mother who had never been married. That's why she never talked about it!" she said in a defensive tone. "And I won't rest until I resolve this once and for all. Since you're a hometown boy, I was wondering if you could help me in my quest."

Declan's eyes widened. "Am I right in assuming that no one in Love knows that your grandmother was born and bred there?"

Annie bit her lip and nodded. "It may seem deceptive, but I really just want to do a little digging before I announce the connection. I could use your assistance."

Declan clenched his jaw. He was clearly mulling over her proposition. Her heart sank. He seemed torn. Finally he answered. "I promise to help you, Annie, but secrets have a way of coming back to bite you," Declan said, a concerned look gracing his handsome face.

"Gram and my mother, God rest their souls, deserve to be acknowledged rather than swept under the rug. If I have to bite my tongue about Gram until I figure it out, then so be it."

She hadn't meant to get on a soapbox, but the fact that two generations of her family had raised children out of wedlock didn't sit well with her. The blame couldn't be heaped solely on them. Part of digging up Gram's past in Love meant making her grandfather accountable for not being in her mother's life and for evading responsibility.

She wasn't going to share that with Declan just yet. She'd already given him enough food for thought.

While Declan stared at her with his mouth hanging open, Annie scooted out of the seat and made her way back across the aisle. She quickly buckled up, then let out a sigh of resolve as she stared out the window at the magnificent Alaskan scenery unfolding before her very eyes. Majestic mountains loomed in the distance. A large body of water—Kachemak Bay, according to her research—glistened with promise. She let out a gasp as the plane began to descend and she spotted eagles circling their nest. Down below she could make out buildings and people and cars.

Excitement roared through her as her dreams merged with reality. Finally, after so many years of dreaming about it, she was moments away from her arrival in Love, Alaska. She felt incredibly blessed. Her life in Alaska was about to begin!

Chapter Five

As the plane went in for its final descent over Kachemak Bay, Annie prepared herself for landing. Twenty-four hours ago she had been involved in a terrifying crash of a similar-size seaplane. It was only natural that she was slightly nervous. As the plane touched down on the water, Annie softly recited a prayer and closed her eyes. Within a few minutes, she realized that the plane had stopped moving. Relief washed over her as she heard Finn announce over the headset that they had arrived in Love.

Thank You, Lord, for safe travels.

After grabbing a few of her belongings, Annie followed right behind Declan as he exited the plane after Boone and Finn. For a moment, she felt disoriented as the glare of the sun hit her squarely in the eyes. She ducked her head, giving herself a moment to adjust to the light. A huge roar sounded all around her. When she looked up, she saw that a huge crowd had assembled by the dock where Ethel had landed.

A beautiful, dark-haired woman, presumably Boone's wife, stood on tiptoe and kissed him on the lips. Her stomach was gently rounded in pregnancy. She then threw her arms around Declan and wiped away tears from her eyes. Finn had radioed ahead to let the authorities know that they had been found alive near the crash site.

It seemed to Annie as if everyone in town was calling out to Declan. There were signs bearing his name, while others simply read Our Hero. Clearly he was beloved by all the villagers. All of a sudden, Declan transformed before her very eyes. He seemed lit up from inside with a lightbulb. White teeth flashed. His shoulders straightened. The sound of his laughter filled the air.

A group of young women swarmed around him. It was almost as if Declan was a rock star or a soldier returning from the battlefield. Who were these women? Declan O'Rourke groupies? Ladies he was dating? A trickle of annoyance flowed through her. Although she wanted to look away from the spectacle they were making of themselves, it was like watching a train wreck. She found herself riveted. There were blondes, brunettes, redheads. Short, tall, brown-skinned, fair-skinned, freckled. Annie shook her head. Declan had his own personal fan club.

She watched as he threw up his hands and chuckled. "Ladies. Ladies. There's enough of me to go around."

Annie rolled her eyes. He was clearly relishing all the attention. She watched on the sidelines as Declan was swept up by a whole new crowd of well-wishers. An older woman wearing a magenta ensemble handed him a teddy bear, and a teenager enthusiastically high-fived him. Although the sight was beautiful to witness, it left her feeling a tad homesick. She had come here to establish a sense of community, but at the moment, she was a stranger. It was a foreign feeling to her and one she didn't enjoy. Her heart sank—until she saw a beautiful sign bearing her name. It read Welcome to Love, Annie. It was feminine and delicate with lots of swirls and flowers and several shades of purple. Declan waved her over and pointed enthusiastically at the sign.

She nodded with approval, smiling at the dark-haired little boy who was holding it up. Annie bent down so that she was on eye level with the cutie-pie. "I really love it." The boy grinned then bowed his head.

"Thanks, Aidan," Declan said, tousling the child's curly hair. The little boy ran off into the crowd.

"Declan O'Rourke!" a raspy voice boomed. Annie felt goose bumps on her arms as a silver-haired older man came into view. "I already had one heart attack. Are you trying to give me another one?" he asked.

"Jasper! Did you miss me?" Declan greeted him with wide-open arms. Annie had sensed before Declan even stated the gentleman's name that she was in the presence of Jasper Prescott.

Jasper wrapped his arms around Declan and embraced him tightly. When they pulled apart, Annie could see tears streaming down Jasper's face. "I promised Killian I would watch over you. Everyone knows you're an honorary member of the Prescott clan. You're just as precious to me as my own grandsons." Jasper's voice radiated affection and an abundance of love.

Declan touched Jasper on the shoulder. "You've always made me feel like one of the fold," he said.

"Grandpa would be proud of that. He thought the world of you."

"I still think of him every day," Jasper said. "He was the truest friend I ever did have."

Annie teared up as she watched the emotional reunion between Jasper and Declan. It was so wonderful to see the two men share such a heartfelt moment. Based on Gram's journal, she already felt a kinship with the mayor of Love. He could possibly be one of the last links to her heritage. If he had been the man to hold Gram's heart in the palm of his hand, he must be quite special. She peered at him, trying to find something in his features that resembled her mother or herself. Hmm. As much as she wanted to see something familiar in his countenance, there wasn't a single feature she could isolate.

"Where's your passenger? Her name is Annie, isn't it? Our new librarian?" Jasper asked in a raised voice. "I'd like to make her acquaintance."

Declan grabbed Jasper's elbow and pulled him in her direction. Jasper's blue eyes twinkled as he gave her the once-over. He tipped his hat to her like an old-fashioned gentleman.

"Jasper, this is Annie Murray, our new librarian," Declan announced with a flourish. "Annie, this is our town mayor, Jasper Prescott."

Jasper reached for her hand and pressed a kiss on her knuckles. "It's my pleasure to welcome you to town. And to tell you how thrilled we all are to have you heading up the new Free Library of Love. This dream has been decades in the making."

All of sudden, when faced with the man who might be her grandfather, Annie felt a bit overwhelmed by the possibilities. Jasper Prescott was a larger-than-life figure from Gram's writings. She had to force words out of her mouth. "Nice to meet you, Mr. Mayor," she murmured. Ugh. Mr. Mayor? Why had she called him that? It sounded ridiculous.

Jasper squeezed her hand. "I'm terribly sorry about the plane crash. You must have been terrified."

Annie darted a glance at Declan. "Let's just say I feel blessed to have made it out safe and sound."

"That's the right attitude, Annie." He eyed her shrewdly. "Are you sure you're not Alaskan? From what Boone just told me, you've shown a great deal of resilience. And fortitude."

She giggled. "Not even the slightest. I was born and bred in Maine in a rather small town named Whimsy," she explained.

Jasper stroked his chin. "Now, why does that sound familiar?" Annie's heart leaped. Perhaps he had a recollection about Gram. Should she just cut to the chase and introduce herself as the granddaughter of Aurelia Alice Murray? Or would it be too abrupt? She didn't want anyone to believe she had come to town with an agenda. Her main goals in relocating to Alaska were to be a participant in Operation Love and to help establish the library. Tracking down her grandfather was important, but she didn't want to alienate the townsfolk right off the bat.

"Don't forget that tomorrow there's a team scheduled to meet you over at the library and help you get everything up and running. They can't wait to get to know you." Jasper winked at her. "I'm sure we'll be seeing each other very soon."

Annie found herself following Jasper with her eyes

as he made his way through the throng of people. There was such a congenial, commanding air about him. Much like Declan, he seemed magnetic. Everyone seemed drawn to him, like moths to the flame. For the umpteenth time, she found herself wondering if Gram, too, had found Jasper Prescott irresistible. Was he her grandfather? Or did the trail lead elsewhere?

Just then a beautiful red-haired woman came rushing to Declan's side. She threw her arms around his neck and said, "I've been praying for your safe return. I'm so tickled that you're in one piece. This town wouldn't be the same without you!"

"Sophie!" Declan cried out. "You have no idea how great it is to see your pretty face." Sophie blushed and said something to Declan that Annie couldn't hear.

Annie swallowed past the hard little lump in her throat. Some things were crystal clear, even to a small-town girl like herself. Declan O'Rourke might be the most handsome man she had ever laid eyes on, but he was also a player extraordinaire. Annie had heard too many cautionary tales about men like him. Gram had given her the drill time after time. *Don't fall for a man simply because he makes your heart race. Don't lose a sense of yourself or your values because you've fallen in love.*

She had forgotten that simple rule once and lived to regret it. That was a mistake she wouldn't be repeating, ever. Not even for sky-blue eyes and cheekbones to die for.

Declan was an appealing, handsome charmer. He had a sense of humor. He was brave. And he lived a life of adventure as a pilot. It was easy to feel a pull toward a man like Declan O'Rourke. But she had to resist the tug she felt in his direction. It was imperative to keep her eyes on the prize. She had relocated to Love, Alaska, in order to live out her dreams and to experience living in her grandmother's hometown. Finding someone to walk through life with was part of the grand adventure. Annie was looking for someone stable and steady. A man who wanted to settle down and make a home and create a family. And give her his name. Despite Declan's endless appeal, he wasn't even close to being the type of guy she needed or wanted in her world. By his own admission, he wasn't looking to ditch his bachelor status.

Annie had a list of things she was striving to accomplish in her new life in Alaska. There was no way in the world that a drop-dead gorgeous pilot was going to sandbag those goals.

Declan drew in a deep breath of air. The scent of fresh catch from the fishing boats hung sharply in the November air. The view from the pier was awe inspiring. White-capped mountains sat majestically in the distance. The waters of Kachemak Bay shimmered as the sun's rays bounced off the waves. This was home sweet home. The plane ride back to Love had been uneventful, if a bit nerve-racking. He had found himself clutching the armrest as Finn headed in for the water landing. The thud he felt when Ethel hit the water seemed more pronounced than usual. And contrary to any emotion he had ever felt before when flying, a trickle of anxiety had settled over him.

Shake it off. This is going to pass like a spring shower, he reassured himself. Flying came as naturally to him as walking. A single incident shouldn't change all that. He just needed some time to decompress.

Boone walked toward him with his arms folded across his chest and a huge grin planted on his face. He looked at Declan and chuckled.

Declan frowned. "What seems to be so hilarious, Sheriff Prescott?"

"Oh, nothing," Boone said. "I just remember standing on this very pier when Grace arrived in town. You asked a lot of questions that day. Now it's my turn to grill you about Annie. The two of you seem to be getting on like a house on fire."

Declan rolled his eyes. "We were stranded together waiting for rescue, Boone. It's not as if we were on a date," Declan said.

"I guess if you're going to be fighting for survival with someone, it might as well be an attractive woman like Annie." Boone leaned in and jabbed him in the side. "Am I right?"

"I guess. But she's more than just a pretty face," Declan said. "She's smart. And resourceful. There's a goodness about her that radiates." Glancing around, he located Annie in the crowd. He couldn't help but smile at the sight of her fuzzy leopard pants.

"Sounds like she's pretty amazing." Boone raised an eyebrow. "Is she special enough to tempt you to put your foot back in the dating pool?"

"I never took my foot out of the dating pool," he cracked. "Declan O'Rourke does just fine in that department."

Boone shook his head. "Come on, Declan. You know what I mean. Connecting with a woman. Finding that special someone. Maybe even settling down. Hint. Hint."

"Someone who completes me?" Declan teased. He held up his hands. "I'm not geared for all that. Don't get me wrong. It's amazing that you found Grace through the Operation Love program, but I'm doing all right the way I am. Matter of fact, I might even have a date tonight."

Boone's jaw went slack. "A date? With who?"

Declan frowned. The name was on the tip of his tongue. What was it again? Caroline? Coraline? He snapped his fingers. "Madeline. She's new in town. One of Jasper's recruits. Prettiest smile you ever saw." The moment the words slipped past his lips, he mentally called himself out. His statement hadn't been true. Annie Murray's smile was the most stunning he had ever seen in his life. But he wasn't about to confess that to Boone. Until he figured out how to deal with these feelings for Annie percolating inside him, he was going to keep things close to the vest.

Declan scoffed, "You married people always want us singletons to follow you down the aisle into wedded matrimony. I'm doing just fine all by myself."

"If you say so," Boone muttered as he walked away shaking his head.

At almost the same time his best friend was leaving in disgust, Annie was walking toward him from the opposite direction. She moved with a pep in her step and a smile plastered on her face. Although he didn't know Annie very well, he had a feeling this was how she navigated her way through life. With optimism and an open heart. He wished he could be more like her. On the inside, where it counted most. He was good at putting on a jovial show, but deep down he had always been nursing his hurts.

"I hope everyone has given you a hearty welcome," Declan said as she stopped beside him.

"I feel like the queen for a day," Annie gushed. "Everyone is so enthusiastic about the library. I really feel that coming here was my destiny." Annie's cheeks were flushed pink with happiness. Her brown eyes sparkled. Her joy was effusive. All of a sudden, he felt excitement building inside him regarding the library. He was beginning to see things through Annie's eyes a little bit. Although he still didn't think the library was a good use of town money, he was happy that Annie was now a resident of Love. But for the library, she would still be back home in Whimsy.

"Love is a great town. It's going to be different from what you're used to. That's for sure. But once it settles inside your heart and mind, you're going to be head over heels for this fishing village. Just you wait and see."

"I'm counting on it. Thanks for everything, Declan," Annie said, an easy grin illuminating her pretty face. "I'm sure we'll run into each other in a town this size, but no matter what happens, please know I'll be eternally grateful for the skill you exercised yesterday and for keeping me in one piece."

"That means a lot," Declan said, overwhelmed by her gratitude. He wasn't quite sure he deserved it, especially since he had no clue why Lucy had been in such distress in the first place. Was there something he had failed to notice in the plane's maintenance checks? Engine failure? He swallowed past his massive doubts. He wouldn't rest until he figured it out. "If you need anything, I'm only a phone call away. Where are you staying?"

"At the Black Bear Cabins. I'm renting one from a woman named Hazel Tookes."

Declan had suspected that, along with a host of other Operation Love participants, Annie would be calling the Black Bear Cabins home. It was where Grace had lived prior to her marriage to Boone. Her best friend, Sophie Miller, a waitress at the Moose Café, still resided there.

"You're in great hands with Hazel. She'll set you up nicely at her cabins. And she makes breakfast for her renters every morning and serves it up at the Lodge, so you're in for a treat. Hazel can really cook!" He rubbed his stomach. "Her blueberry pancakes are my favorite."

"Miss Murray!" a booming voice called out, interrupting their conversation. Declan turned toward the familiar-sounding voice that registered like nails on a chalk board. Dwight Lewis was the town treasurer. At the moment he was hurtling toward them like a rocket. With his round spectacles, his up-to-the knee winter boots and a red bow tie peeping out from underneath his coat, he presented an odd image.

"I just wanted to introduce myself. I'm Dwight Lewis. Town treasurer."

"Call me Annie," she suggested in a chirpy voice. "'Miss Murray' is so formal."

Dwight beamed. He adjusted his glasses and cleared his throat. "Nice to meet you, Annie. I'd like to be the first member of the town council to welcome you to Love."

"Jasper already beat you to the punch," Declan

drawled. He took pleasure in taking the wind out of Dwight's sails. He was such a pompous know-it-all. Dwight stuck his nose in more people's business than a raccoon did scavenging for trash. Declan still hadn't forgiven him for the way he had treated Grace when she had first come to town.

Dwight scowled at him. Score! He'd managed to get under his skin. Declan grinned.

"Well, I hope no one else has brought you flowers." Dwight held out a bouquet of Alaskan fireweed mixed with roses. Declan sucked his teeth. What was Dwight doing? Was he trying to make a play for Annie? Something twisted inside his chest at the thought of Dwight romancing Annie. It wouldn't sit well with him if his hunch was correct.

"Why, thank you, Dwight," Annie gushed, reaching out to accept the bouquet. She raised the flowers to her nose and inhaled deeply, then let out a satisfied sigh. "What a sweet gesture. They're lovely."

"You really landed in Alaska with a bang," Dwight said, his gaze drifting toward Declan. "It's unfortunate that you had to go through such a traumatic experience. My deepest apologies on behalf of the town." Declan scowled. Dwight was making apologies for the plane crash, something he knew nothing about. All Dwight knew was ledgers and bank balances and deposits. What did he know about planes or roughing it in the wilds of Alaska? Clearly he was just looking to score points with Annie.

"Life doesn't always work out the way we think it will," Annie said. "The plane crash was scary, I have to admit." She looked over at him. "But I was in great hands with Declan. We worked together to build a fire and to ensure that we were rescued."

"Well, that must have been interesting, considering the two of you are on opposing sides," Dwight said. He looked back and forth between the two of them.

"Opposing sides? Why do you say that? We got along like biscuits and gravy." The innocent expression on Annie's face made Declan want to punch Dwight in the nose. For as far back as he could remember, Dwight had been a troublemaker. He always seemed to relish opportunities to insert himself into situations and wreak havoc. At the moment, he was stirring the pot with a big spoon.

Dwight smirked at Declan. Right before he opened his mouth, Declan sensed impending danger. He had the feeling that Dwight was about to put all his business out there on full display.

"Well, Declan here was one of the most vociferous opponents of the library." Dwight chuckled. "He lobbied quite vigorously against it." Dwight tapped his finger against his chin. "Correct me if I'm wrong, but if I recall, you said that libraries were dinosaurs and that they would be obsolete ten years from now. You said that not a single penny of this town's money should be allocated toward a building that housed musty old books nobody wants to read."

Declan glared at Dwight. He clenched his fists at his sides. He counted to ten in his head and prayed for self-control. If he had learned one thing from his father's mistakes, it was to think before he acted on raw emotion. Dwight couldn't help being a worm.

Annie gasped and raised her hand to her throat.

She swung her gaze toward him. "Th-that can't be true. Can it?"

He shifted uncomfortably from one foot to the other. "It's not as bad as Dwight here is making it sound," Declan protested. "I was very vocal about town funds being utilized for a new library, but in order to understand, you would have to see it in context. In case you didn't know, this town has been in a recession. We're still in recovery mode. Not to mention that this town did have a library many years ago. It was closed due to lack of funds and ambivalence from the townsfolk."

Annie's narrowed her gaze. There was a sharpness in her eyes that startled him. "So it is true."

Declan sighed. "Yes, it's true. But it wasn't personal, and Dwight is making it sound a lot uglier than it was," he defended himself, flustered by the hurt expression on Annie's face. "I was lobbying against the use of town funding, not against you personally."

"I shared some deeply personal things with you," she said in a wounded voice. "And still you didn't see fit to give it to me straight." Annie's lips trembled, and hurt shone in her eyes. "Without funding, I don't have a job here in Love, and the townsfolk don't have a library," Annie spit out. "And you had plenty of time to tell me this while we were awaiting rescue. If I recall correctly, we even discussed town opposition to the library." Annie let out a harrumph. "You conveniently neglected to mention that you were the opposition."

"I didn't want to get off on the wrong foot with you, Annie," Declan explained sheepishly. "First impressions mean a lot. I didn't want you to think I was a jerk."

Her eyes blazed. Her mouth puckered. "Well, it's too late for that," she snapped as she pivoted on her heel and stormed away from him.

The desire to do bodily harm to Dwight rose up in him sharply and swiftly. He took a step toward him, his movement full of purpose. If he pummeled him, Declan could get all his frustrations out in one fell swoop. The plane crash. Lucy being demolished.

Dwight held up his hands. "It's not my fault you didn't tell her the truth. Don't blame the messenger."

Declan stopped in his tracks. Even though Dwight was a weasel, he was right. He'd had ample opportunity to tell Annie that he had been one of the leading opponents of the Free Library of Love, but he hadn't been able to muster the courage. Something about her left him feeling flummoxed.

It bothered him that Annie had looked at him as if he was beneath contempt. Being liked was important to Declan. He'd worked hard at it for most of his life. Being liked meant he wouldn't be ostracized because of his father and the circumstances surrounding his mother's death. Making jokes and lightening the mood had always been his strong suit. If he could make people see the humorous side of things, it transported him far away from the heavy stuff that threatened to drag him down.

As Dwight scampered away, Declan scoured the area for any sign of Annie. He tried to swallow past the lump in his throat as he watched her being helped into Hazel's van by a group of men from town. He knew every single one of them. They were all bachelors who were participants in Operation Love. The realization made him feel grumpy. As Hazel drove the two of them off into the gorgeous Alaskan afternoon, Declan found his gaze trailing after them.

How in the world was he going to make things right with Annie?

"Welcome to our little Alaskan fishing village, Annie. We're mighty pleased to have you here," Hazel announced from the front seat of the van. Beside her in the passenger seat was a pretty little border collie. The dog had a look on its face that said, "Don't even think about kicking me out of this seat."

"Sorry about the front seat. Astro here is a rescue pet. He insists on riding next to me up here." The silver-haired older woman let out a hearty chuckle. "He thinks he's royalty." Hazel snorted. "He doesn't know yet that he's a mutt."

"It's not a problem, Hazel. I like looking out the window from back here." Annie didn't care where she sat. She felt practically giddy at the notion that her two feet were firmly planted in Love.

As the scenery rushed by, Annie couldn't even focus on all the new sights unfolding before her very eyes. Hazel was giving her a narrative about the town's history, but she simply nodded in response without really listening. Thoughts about Declan had crept in. She was still upset about Declan's opposition to the library. How on earth did someone have the nerve to oppose a library, of all things? Did he have a problem with books? Humph! She had met people like Declan before. Ignoramuses who doubted the need for libraries in their communities. People like him were extremely shortsighted in their thinking. And they had no regard for education. Or the effect libraries had on small children—the next generation.

Annie couldn't remember the last time she had felt so disillusioned about a person. Declan had been so heroic in the forest. Rugged. Appealing. Straightforward. The experience certainly showed her that appearances could be deceiving. Not that she didn't already know that, but this served as a precious reminder that people often wore masks. Sometimes they allowed you to see only what they wanted you to.

She stuffed down a feeling of irritation at the memory of all the young women who had surrounded him at the pier. It wasn't her place to judge but, just as she had suspected, Declan was a magnet for the ladies. She frowned. Why did she even care about his personal life? He was single and fancy-free. Annie didn't care if he dated a dozen women from Operation Love. She wouldn't be one of them!

"Are you hungry?" Hazel asked. "I can make you some lunch up at the Lodge. We're only about five minutes away."

Annie's stomach growled loudly at the mention of food. Hazel let out a chuckle at the sound. "It seems as if your stomach answered the question for me."

She felt her cheeks flush with embarrassment. "I'm famished. Declan and I didn't have much to eat while we were in the forest. The whole time, I was imagining myself biting into a juicy cheeseburger."

"Declan is pretty beloved here in town. I know quite a few women who wouldn't mind being trapped right alongside him." Hazel met her gaze in the rearview mirror and winked.

Annie sniffed. "I wouldn't know anything about that," she said in a crisp voice.

"Uh-oh! What did he do to you? You seem mighty salty about something, if you don't mind my saying so." Hazel's bluntness caught Annie off guard. She seemed like a kindly woman, but she didn't hold back her opinions. Not by a long shot.

"It's nothing," Annie said in a soft voice. "I'm not going to let it bother me."

"Aha. Did he try to kiss you?" Hazel's voice sounded triumphant. "That boy has been charming girls since he was a tadpole."

Annie bristled. "Absolutely not! Declan was a perfect gentleman in every way."

"So you do like him," Hazel said, her tone full of approval. "Most gals do."

Somehow that didn't surprise Annie. Not one little bit.

"He was…fine," Annie admitted. "Until I discovered that he was the one who led the charge against the library funding."

"Oh," Hazel said, drawing out the word. There was understanding in her voice, as if she was fully aware of Declan's position on the Free Library. "We do a lot of debating in this town about how to spend funds. Ever since a recession hit a few years ago, we've had to count every penny. I doubt he meant any harm."

Hazel's explanation slightly mollified her, although she still felt steamed about it. "If he had admitted it once he realized I was the town librarian, I wouldn't be feeling so jaded right now."

"I'm partial to Declan, so I won't say a word against him. That poor boy has been through so much in his life, so forgive me if it seems that I'm giving him a pass." Hazel heaved a tremendous sigh. "I'll admit it. He should have told you."

"What has he been through?" Annie blurted out. Normally she wasn't so nosy, but she wanted to know what forces had made Declan the man he was today. And why did Hazel seem so sad about it?

"His mother died when he was eight." Hazel's eyes held a tortured expression. "His father was incarcerated for almost ten years. Finn and Declan lost their childhood all in one fell swoop."

Annie's stomach twisted painfully. "That's terribly sad," she said. An image of a sweet-faced boy with striking blue eyes popped into her head. She ached for him a little, knowing from experience how hard it was to grow up without parents to guide you.

The O'Rourkes were a family that had been fractured by tragedy and loss and the prison system. Those events must have made a huge impact on Declan's life. She admired him for creating his own business with O'Rourke Charters. It couldn't have been easy, she imagined.

"Killian, their grandfather, raised them all by himself after that. It was a sad day when he passed on," Hazel said in a mournful tone. "Yet another loss for those two."

Hmm. It seemed that she and Declan had something in common, after all. They had both been raised by a grandparent after death, and life circumstances had taken their parents out of the equation. From the sound of it, Declan had endured a lot of loss in his life.

"What about Finn? He really seems to care about Declan."

Hazel sniffed back tears. "He does. In his own way. But Finn has never stuck around Love long enough to even put down roots. Both of them have wounds from losing their mother in such a senseless way. Then, to lose their father to the prison system…the ripples of those events were devastating."

Annie frowned. "What was his father in jail for?"

Hazel made a turning motion on her lips as if she was locking them shut with a key.

"I'm guilty of having a big mouth, Annie," Hazel confessed. "But I wouldn't hurt that boy for all the tea in China. I've said enough. Anything else you want to know about Declan has to come from his lips."

"I understand," Annie said. "I wasn't trying to pry. Blame it on the librarian in me. I'm always seeking answers to the questions rolling around in my head."

"No worries. I was the one who brought it up. In a town like Love, you're bound to find out all the answers to your questions sooner or later. I'd rather not be the one to speak about Colin O'Rourke. It's still a tough subject for the boys."

Boys? Annie might have giggled if the discussion wasn't quite so somber. Declan and Finn were a far cry from boys. They were strapping men who were both extremely easy on the eyes. Alaskan eye candy. Hot men of the tundra. No wonder women were leaving their lives behind and relocating to the far ends of the earth to find love.

"We're here," Hazel announced in a chipper voice as she turned off the main road. A few feet ahead, Annie spotted a rusted, faded sign with a brown bear on it. As soon as Hazel turned onto the private lane, Annie noticed reddish cabins as far as the eye could see. The abundance of snow-covered trees lining either side of the lane reminded her of Maine in winter. There was a quaintness about the area that appealed to her. As Hazel continued down the lane, Annie let out a gasp. A gigantic craggy mountain came into view. It felt as if she could almost reach out and touch it. This, Annie realized, was a sight she would never stop marveling at.

Hazel stopped the car in front of a large, two-story, rustic home. A wooden sign posted in the ground read The Lodge.

Hazel sighed as she stood and looked across at the mountains and the spectacular Alaskan vista. "Beautiful, isn't it? God sure got it right when He created Alaska."

"That's for sure," Annie said. She got out of the car and stood in the clearing, staring off into the distance. There was something so majestic about her surroundings. She inhaled deeply and threw her arms wide. There was no way of knowing whether it had to do with the view or surviving the plane crash, but she suddenly felt more alive than she had in her entire life. Adventure was knocking on her door, and she was going to heed the call.

"Leave your bags in the car. I'll take you back down to the cabins after we get a bite to eat."

Annie followed Hazel as she opened the door to her home and stepped inside. The interior of the Lodge was beautiful. Although Hazel didn't seem like a dainty woman, the furnishings and accents were very feminine and old-fashioned. Annie admired the gleaming hardwood floors and stained glass windows. Gorgeous paintings of Alaskan landscapes adorned her walls. A velvet settee, a mahogany armoire and a glass-front china cabinet all added special touches that lent the place an understated elegance.

"Why don't you sit down and relax while I heat up the food. The powder room is right down the hall if you're so inclined." Hazel's kindness was making Annie feel at home, despite experiencing a few pangs of homesickness. Everything was so different here! Even though she had craved this Alaskan adventure, it was still a bit nerve-racking to step out of your comfort zone and embrace change.

If you always do what you always did, then life would be pretty boring, wouldn't it? Another Gramism popped into her head, serving as a reminder that she needed to be brave. Her new life in Alaska was a journey of discovery. Isn't that what she had wanted?

She looked around the room, noticing all the pictures. A framed photo of Hazel and Jasper sat on a side table.

"Is Jasper your boyfriend?" Annie asked as soon as Hazel returned. Judging by the picture of the two of them, they looked as if they were more than friends.

"That depends on what day it is," Hazel cracked. She shook her head and let out a boisterous laugh. "Just teasing. Jasper is my honey bear. We've been together for about a year now."

"That's wonderful, Hazel," Annie gushed.

"I loved him from afar for quite some time. Jasper finally got his act together and showed he had some common sense," Hazel said in a crisp voice.

Annie was intrigued by the idea of a romance between the older couple. It was sweet that they had found love with one another later in life. She wished

Gram had found someone special to pass the time with in her golden years. It was sad to think that, other than a youthful relationship, she had never experienced romantic love. *I don't need a man in my life when I have you,* Gram had always said. Annie had never believed her.

Gram. The ache of loss still tugged at her heartstrings relentlessly. Annie had hoped that coming to her grandmother's hometown would serve as a healing balm for her sorrow. But grief was a process that she had to walk through one step at a time. As important as her grandmother had been to her during her lifetime, it was only fitting that she would miss her like crazy.

"Come sit down at the table," Hazel instructed. "The grub is piping hot and ready to be served." Hazel ushered Annie into the dining room, where two places had been set. In the middle of the table were platters of food—chicken, a rice dish and biscuits and gravy.

"What an amazing spread," Annie said as she inhaled the delectable scent of Hazel's down-home cooking. Hazel reached for her plate and began to heap a generous helping of the food onto her dish.

"I cooked this morning for you in anticipation of your arrival. I knew the rescuers would find you and Declan. Praise the Lord!" Hazel raised her palms in the air.

Annie dug into her food. "He had our backs the whole time," she said with a nod. Despite her fear, she had known that God was watching over them. They had been under His protection the entire time. That was the real blessing.

They enjoyed a companionable silence as they

ate the food Hazel had prepared. Sitting down for a meal at Hazel's table allowed Annie to feel the sweet warmth of home. Sunday dinners at Gram's table had always been a festive affair. Each week she would hand-select members of their congregation to break bread with them at their home. The table would be laden with too many dishes to count—ham, mashed potatoes, macaroni and cheese, chicken and salad. Over the dining room table they had enjoyed fellowship and laughter and the best food in all of Maine. Those get-togethers had filled their house with so much light and love that her heart overflowed. If it was possible to go back and gather those memories in a bottle to preserve them for all time, she would do it in a heartbeat. What she wouldn't give for one more day with Gram. Or simply to hear her tinkling laughter ring out.

"There are plenty of other gals staying here at the cabins. All of 'em came to town as participants in Operation Love," Hazel explained. "Nice bunch of ladies. A few already found their fellas and are planning weddings or have tied the knot."

Weddings! "Wow. That's exciting," Annie said. "How many have gotten married?"

Hazel looked up at the ceiling for a moment. Her lips were moving, and Annie could tell she was counting in her head. "Since this whole program began, I think there have been five marriages. It's really hard to keep up with all the engagements." Her mouth quirked. "There have been a few breakups, too."

"That's only natural, I imagine. Declan told me about Boone and his wife."

Hazel's face lit up. "Grace! What a sweetheart.

Boone and Grace were the first couple to get married as a result of Operation Love. Jasper was sure tickled about his grandson being part of the inaugural couple.

"Do you have a type, Annie? I might be able to steer you in the right direction," Hazel said with a grin. "We've got a lot of good, faith-driven men here in Love. And some of 'em are mighty cute."

Declan's face popped into her mind. She did her best to stuff down all visions of Declan threatening to flash before her eyes. What woman wouldn't envision him as her type?

Tall. Easy on the eyes. Funny. A sigh slipped past her lips. She didn't need to set her sights on a confirmed bachelor, particularly one who seemed to be a magnet for every single woman in town.

"A type? Not exactly," she answered. "As far as looks go, I'm open to all types. I don't want a lady's man, though."

Hazel leaned in a little bit across the table. "Sounds like you've been burned before. Am I right?"

Annie didn't like to share her romantic past with people. It made her feel foolish to admit that she had been played for a fool in the game of love. But something in Hazel's sympathetic gaze encouraged her to open up. "Yes. It's true. A few years back, I was dating someone who turned out to be quite unscrupulous. He was seeing several young ladies throughout the state of Maine, all the while telling each one of us he was true-blue."

"What a cad!" Hazel said angrily. "How did it all end?"

Annie's cheeks felt flushed. It was hard dredging up her disastrous romance with Todd Wenkelman. She tried her best never to think about him and his duplicity. Her first and only romantic relationship had ended in a grand deception. "His fiancée showed up at my door, and the jig was up. She was tracking down all his girlfriends so she could expose him. There was even a story in the newspaper about him and how he had duped so many women. They called him 'the lying lothario.'"

Hazel reached across the table and patted Annie's hand. "Rest assured, Annie. You won't find anyone like that here in Love. If any man ever acted like that, we'd run him out of town on a rail."

Fatigue was beginning to seep into her bones. Although she had slept last night, it hadn't been a restful slumber, thanks to the bat drama and anxiety about being rescued.

Hazel made a tutting sound. "You look beat. After all you've been through, rest is the best medicine."

"I can't argue with that, Hazel. I think the fading sunlight is confusing me a bit. It feels much later than it actually is."

"Let me drive you down to your cabin. Sorry that you won't be able to sleep in tomorrow morning, but if we're going to get the library up and running, we'll have to start working on it bright and early. I'm part of the set-up team."

"No problem," Annie said in a chirpy voice. "I'm used to it. Librarian hours. And it will all be worth it when we can open our doors to the community."

Hazel drove her down to her cabin. Annie let out a squeal as she spotted the pretty sign with her name on it, accompanied by streamers and stuck to her front door.

"Sophie did all that for you. She lives a few doors

down from you. Sweeter gal you'll never find if you're looking for a friend," Hazel said.

After giving Hazel a tight hug and taking her keys, Annie went about the business of settling in. Her cabin was no frills. The decor was varying shades of brown. The couch looked sturdy, and the bed seemed pretty comfortable. The trunks of clothes she had sent ahead weeks ago sat in her new bedroom waiting to be unpacked. Thankfully she had shipped some items from home that would jazz up her place. A living room rug. A cozy comforter. Her Gram's quilt would look right at home at the end of her bed. By the time she added her own personal touches to the cabin, it would resemble something from a vintage-chic magazine.

After she unpacked her belongings, then switched to her pajamas to head off to an early slumber, she remembered to say her prayers. Despite all the drama she had endured to get to this wonderful town, there was still so much to be thankful for.

Thank You for getting me here safely, Lord. And for being by my side throughout the ordeal. Although I'm still mad at Declan for trying to stand in the way of my library, please keep watch over him. He took care of me and made me feel safe when I might have fallen apart otherwise.

As Annie bundled up under the covers and laid her head down on her pillow, she willed herself to stop thinking about Declan O'Rourke. Yes, he was gorgeous and funny and heroic. But she had no intention of getting involved with a playboy who had the ability to charm all the ladies in town.

She had come to this quaint village to find the love of her life—a true-blue guy who would make an excellent husband for her. She didn't need the likes of Declan O'Rourke messing up her plans.

After leaving the pier, Declan headed straight home to the log cabin where he had grown up. It was about ten minutes from town, with a clear view of Deer Run Lake and the mountains. He took a moment to stand in his yard and survey the property. It had come a long way since he had inherited it from his grandfather Killian O'Rourke. Being good with his hands had allowed Declan to make the renovations on the house without breaking the bank. With a new roof, updated cedar log siding and the addition of a front porch, he now owned a home that was rustic, up-to-date and functional.

Before he knew it, there was a banging sound on his front door. Without waiting for an answer, Finn let himself in. He had a duffel bag slung over his shoulder.

"Hey, I need a place to crash for a while."

"Define 'a while,'" Declan said. This was typical Finn. He'd breeze into town for a few weeks, then disappear as soon as the mood struck him. It drove Declan nuts. Just once he would have liked to see his brother stay in one place long enough to connect.

"I'm thinking about moving back here for good," Finn said. "Maybe find some work here in town and get a place to fix up and make my own." He placed his bag down with a thud.

Declan let out a groan. "Finn. We've been down this road before. Each and every time, you bail on the plan."

Finn scowled. "I knew you were going to be negative."

"With good reason. If I had a dollar for every time you announced you were moving back here, I'd have enough money to buy another plane to replace Lucy."

He hadn't meant to bring up Lucy, but he was still smarting over the fact that she was gone forever. Nothing more than a pile of wreckage and ash.

"Have you contacted the insurance company yet?" Finn asked. "O'Rourke Charters is going to be in a bind if you don't get a second plane. It's really helped the company financially to have Willard making some runs for you."

Willard Jones was a local pilot who was in Declan's employ. Even though Willard had only gotten his pilot's license last year, he demonstrated great skill and ability. Declan wasn't looking forward to telling him about Lucy's demise.

"I need to call them," Declan said sheepishly. "There might be a slight hiccup since I lowered my premium last year. The payout from the insurance company won't be enough to finance a new plane."

"You did what?" Finn exploded. He began to grind his teeth noisily. "Why in the world did you do a thing like that?"

"Love was in a recession. O'Rourke Charters took a real beating," he drawled. "Oh, I forgot. You didn't stay in town long enough to experience the hardships firsthand."

"We've both experienced tough times. There's no need to compare battle scars," Finn spit out.

An uneasy silence stretched between them. Things left unspoken pulsed in the air. It was always like this between them, Declan realized. Everything could be going swell until the past reared its head like a monster. He was beginning to think they would never be able to cross the divide that separated them.

"You're just like him. You can never just stay put in one place. Even when Grandpa was sick, you couldn't just plant roots here, could you?" Declan asked.

"I'm not like him!" Finn let out a snort. "You're the one who flits from one woman to the next. Sound familiar?"

Declan felt as if he had been sucker punched in the gut. Finn really knew how to hit below the belt.

Finn raked his hands through his hair. "I shouldn't have said that."

Declan clenched his fists and moved toward his brother. All he could see was a red haze. Before he did something he regretted, he bent down and picked up Finn's duffel bag and tossed it at him. "You can't stay here!"

They locked gazes. It seemed like an eternity passed before Finn spoke. "Fine. I'll go crash somewhere else. Maybe when you talk to the insurance company, you can blame me for everything, just like you always do." Like a whirlwind, Finn left his house. The roaring sound of his motorcycle buzzed in Declan's ears. He wanted to go after him to tell him he could stay, but a heavy weight on his chest prevented him from doing so. Too much stood between them.

Like always, the past had crept into his present, bringing along with it things he knew neither one of them was capable of facing.

Chapter Six

Annie was up at the crack of dawn, well before she needed to wake up. A feeling of anticipation had been building inside her ever since her arrival in town a week earlier. For the past seven days, she had been working toward getting the library in shipshape condition, shelving and unpacking books.

She couldn't have done it without the dedicated team who had helped her get the library in order. And even though there were still a few things that needed to be straightened out, the library was officially opening this morning with a ribbon-cutting ceremony to celebrate the grand achievement. Townsfolk would be able to come to the library, sign up for a library card and actually take books out. All the books from the original library had been moved to the site and shelved right alongside the new books.

She was filled with anticipation. It reminded her of how she had always felt the night before the first day of school—brimming with excitement. *New beginnings are always ripe with possibilities.* Hadn't she just read that very phrase in Gram's journal?

Even though she could have slept for another hour or so, Annie's internal clock wouldn't allow her to. She considered herself to be a very punctual person, and she didn't want to run the risk of being late for the ceremony. In her position as librarian at the Whimsy Public Library, punctuality had been a necessity. It was her responsibility to open up the library each and every morning so patrons could have access. Not once had the library ever opened late. That was because she was an organized person. She was quite proud of her impeccable record with regard to the operating hours of the library. It was nothing to sneeze at. And she had every intention of continuing that legacy right here in Love.

Annie got up out of bed and walked into the living room. She pulled back the dark curtains and peered outside. "Hello, beautiful Alaska," she gushed. Pink and purple ribbons of color streaked across the sky. Annie found herself transfixed by the sight of God's wondrous creation. The sun was creeping over the horizon, its fiery brilliance heralding a new day. Mountains loomed majestically in the distance. She had done her research on Alaska. She knew that sunset would occur at around five o'clock later on today, a little bit later than she was used to back home. For now she would simply bask in the beautiful sunrise unfolding right outside her window.

Hazel wasn't coming by to pick her up for another hour or so. She had declined breakfast at the Lodge due to the butterflies fluttering in her stomach. Who could eat when a new library was being celebrated? For the past week she had been assembling the li-

brary's catalog with help from a group of townsfolk
who were big supporters.

After taking a shower, Annie got dressed and did
her makeup and hair. She put on a light dusting of
powder, followed by a hint of black eyeliner and mas-
cara. The final touch was a slash of red on her lips.
Retro red, she liked to call it. She had curled her hair
so that it hung in waves. One look in the mirror had
Annie convinced she could put her best foot forward
at the ceremony. Her outfit was as close to perfection
as she could imagine. She had purchased the gray
wool dress at a vintage shop on a trip to Bar Harbor.
Her plaid coat with the faux-fur collar completed the
outfit. She pulled on her tall brown boots and inhaled
a deep, steadying breath.

A quick glance at her watch revealed that Hazel
would be arriving in a matter of minutes. When she
flung open the front door of the cabin so she could
wait outside on the porch, she saw a big box sitting at
her doorstep. Hmm. She hadn't ordered anything, nor
was she expecting a delivery from back home. Perhaps someone had left it at the wrong cabin. When she
picked it up, she noticed a small tag with her name on
it taped to the box. It read "For Annie." Nope. There
hadn't been a delivery mistake. Had someone from
Whimsy sent her a care package? If so, she hoped
it was full of treats from her favorite candy store in
town, Betsy's Penny Candy. She bent down and ripped
it open, letting out a sigh as a pair of snow-white boots
came into view. A cream-colored card sat perched on
top of them.

Just wanted to make sure your toes never get cold again. Declan.

She ran her fingers across the handwritten note as a surge of joy rose up inside her. She had truly missed seeing him over the past week. And then out of the blue he'd sent her the boots! It was one of the most thoughtful things anyone had ever done for her.

The words written by Declan went straight to her heart. Even though she hadn't yet forgiven him, the thoughtful gift served as a huge incentive to patch things up with him. She carried the box back inside her cabin and switched the boots she was wearing with the Lovely boots. The moment her feet slid inside the warm, cozy shoes, she let out a sigh of contentment. They were perfect to wear to the ceremony. And they matched her outfit.

When she heard the toot of Hazel's horn, she grabbed her purse and rushed to the door. Today was the first day of the rest of her life. As she delicately navigated the snowy path, she felt very thankful for her Lovely boots. The pair she'd brought from home would have had her slipping and sliding. These new ones provided great traction on the snow and ice.

Once again, Declan had stepped in and rescued her.

Declan hadn't planned on attending the ribbon-cutting ceremony for the library. He had plenty of business to square away today as a result of the plane crash. For the past week he had been dealing with insurance issues, rearranging the schedule and trying to deal with his flying jitters. Getting O'Rourke Charters back on track was his number one priority. It was critical! He had to admit that he had been motivated to show up today by a simple desire to see Annie again and to find out if the boots had placed him back in her good graces.

As soon as he arrived, he made a beeline toward Boone, Grace, Jasper and Hazel. Boone and Grace were holding hands and making goo-goo eyes at each other. Declan shook his head. Boone and his brother Cameron both were newly married and besotted with their wives. He had to give it to them. They did make marriage seem like a blissful state of being.

Declan casually scanned the crowd, hoping for a sighting of Annie.

"If you're looking for our new librarian," Boone said, pointing his finger toward the building, "she just went inside for a moment."

"I wasn't looking for anyone in particular. Just checking things out. There's a nice crowd here," he said, quickly veering the subject away from Annie.

Grace grinned. "I think everyone is curious about the new library, as well as Love's newest transplant."

Declan cast a quick glance at his watch. The ribbon-cutting ceremony was scheduled to take place in ten minutes on the front steps of the library. The library was a small brick building on Frontier Street that had formerly been the post office. When the post office had been upgraded to a bigger building, the former site had been left vacant. It was a decent size, and with a little spit and polish, it exuded a quaint charm. According to Boone and the rest of the members of the town council, it would be a work in progress.

Now it was going to house a collection of books, movies, periodicals and audiobooks. Declan himself had never been much of a reader, although he did find the subject of aviation history a fascinating one. Maybe he would see if the library had any books like that on the shelves.

All of a sudden he caught a flash of her gray dress set against dark hair. Annie! Declan didn't think he'd ever been speechless a day in his life, but at the moment all he could do was gawk at the beautiful woman standing on the library steps. *Radiant* was the first word that came to mind.

"Doesn't she look lovely?" Hazel asked, sidling up next to Declan.

"She sure cleans up well," Jasper marveled. "Reminds me of one those old-fashioned movie stars we grew up watching on the silver screen. She looks downright regal."

Boone folded his arms across his chest and rocked back on his heels. "I can only imagine what kind of a stir she's going to make in this town," he marveled. He leaned over and placed a kiss on his wife's forehead. "Kind of like someone else I know."

Grace shook her head and chuckled. "I only had eyes for you."

Declan didn't trust himself to comment. Boone's statement didn't sit well with him. His throat felt a little dry. He fought to speak past the lump in his throat.

For a man who had been crushing on girls since kindergarten, feeling off-kilter like this was out of the ordinary. Just like Annie Murray herself.

"She's beautiful inside and out," Hazel declared. She sent Declan a knowing look. "She'll make a mighty fine wife for someone in this town."

"You're about as subtle as a sledgehammer, Hazel.

The last thing I need is a wife," Declan said. "And we all know it."

"I know no such thing," Hazel quipped.

"People were meant to be partnered up, two by two," Jasper groused. "Get on with it already. If the new librarian doesn't float your boat, there are plenty of other single ladies you can court."

"What about you?" Declan asked, jutting his chin in Jasper's direction. "When are the two of you getting hitched?"

Jasper's eyes bulged and he began to stammer. "M-marriage is for young folks, not old roosters like Hazel and myself."

Hazel let out a shocked gasp. She drew herself up to her full height and began breathing deeply in and out of her nose. "Jasper Prescott! You may consider yourself an old rooster, but I don't think of myself in those terms." She bristled. "I may not be a spring chicken, but I'm not ready yet to be put out to pasture."

Before Jasper could say a word, Hazel stomped off. Boone and Declan tried to stifle their laughter behind their hands. Grace jabbed her husband in his side. Jasper sent them a fierce glare. "Thanks a lot," he griped as he walked after her. Declan subtly tried to locate Annie again in the crowd. He felt Boone's gaze on him. Boone's lips were twitching with merriment.

"What?" he snapped. "You look like the cat that swallowed the cream."

"Take a picture. It might last longer," Boone said with a straight face that suddenly dissolved into a grin threatening to take over his entire face.

"You're a regular comedian, aren't you?" Declan drawled. Almost a year ago, he had said those same words to Boone when he'd caught him staring at Grace in the Moose Café, the coffee bar owned by his brother Cameron Prescott. Boone's mind was like a steel trap. He never forgot a single thing.

"Go on and talk to her. You know you want to," Boone said in a singsong voice.

Declan rolled his eyes and shook his head as he walked away from his best friend. Boone's hearty chuckle trailed after him. With every step he took toward Annie, he became more nervous. Not seeing Annie for the past week had been like not catching a glimpse of the sun.

He didn't have any idea what was wrong with him, considering making small talk with women was his strong suit.

She met his gaze from where she stood on the steps. He studied her expression, but it didn't tell him anything about whether or not she'd forgiven him. For once, her features were closed off. She looked unapproachable. He placed his hand over his chest, startled by the pounding of his heart.

Annie's shoulder-length hair now hung in loose waves, gently framing her face and gleaming like burnished wood. Every time she moved her head, it swung around her shoulders. Her dress peeked out from under her coat. It resembled something from another era. It was a really nice shade of gray. It hung past her knees and showcased her great sense of style. On the side of her head sat a black hat with some netting and a little bird on it. Or at least, he thought it was a hat. It looked a tad unusual, although Annie managed to pull it off.

"Hey there, Annie." His eyes slid down to her feet

and the boots he'd bought for her. A ridiculous amount of joy speared through him at the sight of her wearing his gift. It made him feel ten feet tall. How mad could she still be at him if she was sporting the peace offering?

Her smile showcased dimples he hadn't noticed before. "Thank you for the boots. I love them," she said, flexing her right foot to show off the shoes.

Relief flooded him. "I'm glad you like them. They look great on you."

"That's what Hazel said when she came to pick me up. I can't believe she created these boots and the town developed them as a way to boost revenue." She shook her head and laughed. "It's fairly mind-boggling."

"That's our Hazel. She's one of a kind. And those boots of hers have been helping the economy here in town," Declan said.

Annie grinned. "Anything that helps the economy is a wonderful thing indeed."

Declan stuffed his hands in his pockets. "I wasn't sure if you'd still be speaking to me."

Annie locked gazes with him. "I'm a big believer in forgiveness. You wouldn't be here today if you didn't support the library, now would you?" She gifted him with a beatific smile. "That's good enough for me."

"Maybe I just believe in you," he blurted out. All of a sudden, he felt as if his defenses were down. He had hoped Annie would forgive him, but he hadn't counted on the way it would make him feel to see her again or to realize how easily she could twist him up inside. He'd spent the past week keeping his distance from her, knowing that it was for the best. Being in her presence made him feel as if he was on a high wire without a safety net.

One false move and he might just fall on his face.

Annie's cheeks started to feel warm despite the November chill, and she looked down at the ground to avoid the intensity of Declan's stare. When she swung her gaze back up to meet his scrutiny, she reminded herself to remain unflappable. Declan had an uncanny ability to shake her composure. It wasn't just his good looks, she realized. He made her feel more alive than she had ever felt in her life. Suddenly everything around her seemed more vibrant. The sky was now a more vivid shade of blue. Cerulean. The sound of the red-breasted bird rang out more sweetly when she was in his presence. And knowing he thought well of her calmed down all her jitters about the ribbon-cutting ceremony.

"If you're trying to flatter me, it's working. Don't stop there," she said in a light tone. "Keep 'em coming."

"Well, for starters, you're the prettiest librarian I've ever seen," Declan said. He smiled at her, appreciation evident in his gaze.

She shook her head, not quite believing him. "Am I the only librarian you've ever seen?" she asked.

"Of course you're not." Declan frowned. "I'm not some local yokel who's never left Alaska. I've lived a little. I'm sure you're used to being told you're stunning."

Not exactly, she wanted to say. She deliberately let Declan's statement sit out there unanswered. The truth was, she wasn't used to flattery or sweet words about her looks. Other than her ill-fated romance with Todd, she had barely dated. *Once bitten, twice shy.*

Annie couldn't stop smiling. His compliments meant more to her than she wanted to admit to herself. She had missed being in his presence over the past week. In such a short time he had grown on her, and not seeing him had caused an ache inside her. She'd even wondered if Declan had been avoiding her.

It had been a long time since a man had told her she was attractive. And hearing it from his lips made her want to do cartwheels. There was something about Declan that was so endearing, even when she felt annoyed at him. It scared her a little bit that he had so easily crept past the defenses she had worked hard to build up.

And she worried that it meant so much to her to hear his sweet words. After all, Declan could never be more than a good friend. That knowledge felt bittersweet, but she knew it with a deep certainty.

She waved her hand at him. "Enough with the flowery words. You agreed to help me find the missing pieces from my family tree, so I can't very well stop speaking to you."

"Phew." Declan wiped his hand across his forehead in an exaggerated gesture. "I'm glad I agreed to help you," he said in a teasing tone.

She had no intention of allowing him to get off too easily, considering everything that was at stake. "But I can't forget that we're on opposite sides as far as the funding for the library is concerned," she admitted.

"We may not agree on that issue, but please know that I'm always going to be rooting for you."

"I appreciate you saying so, Declan." Annie looked

around at the crowd. "Everyone has been so encouraging about the library. And the library's board of directors is very confident about getting more funds to support full-time hours. Dwight told me that there are upcoming fund-raisers to support the endeavor." Her eyes twinkled. "He mentioned an ice-skating event at Deer Run Lake and a bake-off in the spring."

"If I were you, I'd watch out for Dwight," Declan leaned in and whispered in her ear.

"Why? He seems as harmless as a fly."

"The man cannot be trusted. I'm not supposed to tell anyone, but do you know that he used to rob little old ladies of their purses?" Declan nodded his head at her, his expression somber.

Annie let out a whoop of laughter, then clapped her hand over her mouth. Declan reached out and removed her hand. "Don't do that. Laughter should be shared. It's one of the best sounds in the universe."

She giggled. "That is not true about Dwight. You just made that up."

Declan grinned. "I admit it. I did make it up. I had to get him back somehow for trying to turn you against me."

"That's not possible. Not after what we went through together." She waved a finger at him. "But I am determined to make you see the value of a library. Every town needs one."

"I'll take your word for it," Declan scoffed.

"Knowledge is the key to life," Annie said in her chirpiest voice. "Books unlock the world."

"I guess I'm a graduate of the school of hard knocks. Everything I've learned in my life has come about through actual hands-on experience." He shrugged.

"I never went to college. I graduated high school by the skin of my teeth. But I aced every test I needed to in order to get my pilot's license. That's how badly I wanted to soar."

From the sound of it, Declan had been living his life out loud. That's what she wanted for herself. Adventures. Romance. A life beyond the walls of her beloved library. To reach out for that brass ring and grab hold of it for all she was worth.

"Ladies and gentlemen," Jasper's voice rang out, interrupting their conversation. "Welcome to the official opening of the Free Library of Love." He gestured to Annie to join him on the library steps. Annie scurried over to stand next to Jasper, and the town-council members assembled around him. "I'd like to introduce you to our newest resident, Annie Murray. With her leadership and vision, the residents of Love are going to have the best library in all of Alaska." The crowd began to applaud loudly. Jasper turned toward Annie and held out the scissors. "I'd like to give you the honor of cutting the ribbon on this most auspicious day." Annie took the scissors from Jasper's hand.

Turning toward the crowd, Annie began to speak. "Thank you for entrusting me with this wonderful treasure. And a special thanks to everyone who helped me get this place organized. Sometimes it does take a village. I'm looking forward to every minute of being a librarian here in Love. Most of all, I'm very excited about getting to know all of you and introducing you to your next favorite book." Annie held up the scissors and cut the ribbon. She blinked back tears.

It felt so gratifying to be standing here in Gram's hometown on the precipice of something wonderful.

Her gaze wandered to Declan in the crowd. He smiled at her. It felt as if she had been jolted by an electrical bolt. The feeling caught her off guard.

Dear Lord, please protect me from wishing for things that I know are way out of my reach. Declan O'Rourke may be the most fascinating man in all of Alaska, but he's also the very last thing I need.

The Free Library of Love wasn't so bad, as far as Declan could tell. It was bright and cheery inside. White walls with vivid splashes of color like an artist's palette. Children's artwork intermingled with pictures of the Alaskan landscape. Cozy couches and love seats were scattered around the interior. Balloons floated in the air, a celebratory touch that added a bit of whimsy to the day.

Declan wandered around the library, checking out the shelves, and searched the catalog in the computer. As he walked past the children's room, he couldn't resist stepping inside the moment he saw the scene taking place. Watching Boone's four-year-old nephew, Aidan, being read to by his father warmed Declan's insides. Dr. Liam Prescott had suffered the tragic loss of his beautiful wife, Ruby, two years ago. Since that time, Liam had struggled to get past his grief, all while raising his young son. Only recently had Liam reopened his medical practice and emerged from his solitude.

"Aidan sure looks happy," Declan remarked.

"He loves books," Liam said, looking up at Declan. "I can't keep enough in the house to quench his thirst. At this rate, he's going to be an early reader." Pride radiated from Liam's voice.

"That's great, A-man," Declan said, holding up his hand so Aidan could give him a high-five. The little boy slapped his hand, then went right back to reading his book with his father. Declan had to chuckle. He didn't think he'd ever seen Aidan so engrossed in anything. Despite everything they had endured, there was a tight bond between father and son. Given his fractured relationship with his own dad, he envied the loving nature of their relationship. Seeing them together made him question his opposition to the library. If it could create something so heartwarming and wonderful for the people he loved, who was he to stand in its way?

"Grace and Boone are going to get a lot of mileage out of this place," Liam said with a wide grin.

Declan hadn't even thought about that. With Grace due to give birth to their first child at the beginning of the new year, she and Boone would both be seeking out advice on child-rearing as well as seeking out picture books to keep their little one entertained. "They sure will," he agreed, swallowing past the feeling of shame rising up inside him. Once he'd met Annie and discovered that she was Love's librarian, he had felt the first stirrings of regret about opposing the library. He had lobbied against this very place, and now that he was standing inside it and seeing it firsthand, he realized how wrong he'd been. And he was going to make sure everyone on the town council knew that he'd had a change of heart. He still had an eye on the town's financial well-being and he would still continue to do so, but he no longer felt absolute certainty about his previous position regarding the library funding.

He began walking toward the exit, feeling enlightened by everything he'd been exposed to this morning.

Annie rushed toward him. "Declan! Are you leaving?"

"I've got some things to straighten out about the plane crash. An investigation is underway into the cause of it. They need to interview me," he explained. "If this comes back as pilot error, that could put O'Rourke Charters out of business. I'd lose a lot of clients if I had that on my record." Not to mention he still had to wade through insurance issues regarding the payout for replacing Lucy. He was feeling antsy about the fate of O'Rourke Charters. His whole future depended on this investigation and getting another plane. Operating O'Rourke Charters with just one plane would severely impact his revenue. And if he didn't get over his sudden reluctance to fly, his company would be toast.

"If you need me to vouch for you, I will. You saved both of our lives."

Annie's encouragement gave him a boost.

"You're still going to help me with my special project, aren't you?" she asked.

"Of course I will, Annie. I know how important it is to you to find your roots." He narrowed his gaze. "I'm still a little dubious as to how you're going to accomplish it, but judging by your enthusiasm, something tells me you're going to convince me."

"Can we meet up tomorrow?" she asked, eagerness etched on her pretty face. "I'll bring Gram's journal and some notes I've taken."

"I have a client I'm taking to Kodiak in the morning, and then I need to fill out some paperwork about

Lucy, but I could meet you at the Moose Café at noon."
He prayed that he could summon the strength to get
past his flying jitters and make the run tomorrow.

"I've seen the place, but I haven't eaten there yet,"
Annie said. "I've been brown bagging it for lunch."

"Cameron sure knew what he was doing when he
opened it. It's only a five-minute walk from here, and
it serves some of the best food in town." He would
never admit it to Annie, but he was a bundle of nerves
about tomorrow's flight to Kodiak. His first time up
in the air after the crash would be tense.

"That's great! I'll see you tomorrow," she said with
a grin before turning back toward Aidan and Liam.
She sat down beside the child and opened a book in
her lap. Just the sight of the three of them made the
wheels in his head turn. Liam was the type of guy
Annie should be matched up with in Operation Love.
Liam was stable and hard-working and dedicated to
hearth and home. He had been an excellent husband
to Ruby. Annie deserved someone who could give her
a wedding ring and promises of forever.

Something had tugged at his insides at the sight
of her so overcome with emotion during the ribbon-
cutting ceremony. He didn't know why he was feeling
such a kinship with Annie. Perhaps it was the plane
crash. Maybe it was the way she seemed to embrace
the world and all it had to offer. Perhaps it was because she was unlike any other woman he had ever
known.

Who was he kidding? The idea of her settling down
with any bachelor in Love left him twisted up inside.
It gnawed at him. And he couldn't quite put his finger
on why it left him feeling so gutted.

All he knew for certain was that she was starting to make him think about things he had stopped hoping for a long time ago.

Chapter Seven

For Declan, walking into the Moose Café was always a pleasurable experience. It was his haven from the day-to-day hustle and grind. And because of Cameron's establishment, he had discovered that he really enjoyed lattes and the fancy coffee drinks that a person almost needed a degree to order. Tongue twisters, he called them. Boone teased him all the time about it, but he really was becoming a coffee connoisseur. Lately the café had expanded its menu to include mouth-watering sandwiches, soups, baked goods, pizza and a handful of entrées. He let out a chuckle. If he could afford it, he would eat every meal here.

The moment he walked in, he was met with unbridled enthusiasm by a few regulars.

"Here's our ace pilot. I've been saying it all week, Declan. You're a real hero! One of these days I'm going to let you take me up in the wild blue yonder with you," a deep voice greeted him.

Declan paused in his tracks to say hello to two older white-haired gentlemen who were seated together at a table.

"Hey, Eli. Zachariah. How are you guys doing?" he asked, stopping beside their usual table.

"Doing pretty well. Can't complain," Eli quipped. "The good Lord woke me up this morning, so as far as I'm concerned, it's a great day indeed." Eli's brown eyes radiated joy.

"I can complain," Zachariah said in a cranky tone. His nose looked pinched as if he had just smelled something foul. "We're still waiting for our grub. I'm not getting any younger sitting around here."

"Look on the bright side," Eli suggested. "At least you don't have to eat by your lonesome. I'm a great conversationalist."

"I'd much rather eat with a female dining companion," Zachariah grumbled. "I've got a bone to pick with Jasper about all these young women coming to Love. When is the senior set going to be matched up with women in our age group?"

"Good point, Zach. You've still got a little life in you yet." Eli laughed heartily.

"If Jasper can get a girl, I shouldn't be sitting around like a wallflower," Zachariah said with a frown. "You've got Cilla."

Declan tried not to laugh. Eli and Zachariah were cronies of Jasper. Eli had been happily married to his sweetheart since they were in their late teens. The three of them, along with his own grandfather, Killian, had grown up in each other's pockets. They had formed a tight circle of friendship that went all the way back to their toddler years. When Jasper joined up with them, it was a rib-tickling, hilarious spectacle.

"Enjoy your lunch, boys," Declan said as he made his way toward a table in the back. If Annie wanted to discuss her grandmother's diary entries, she might want a little privacy. *Poor Annie*, he thought. She was clearly trying to fill a void after losing her beloved Gram. Latching on to the idea of finding a family member here in town was a direct result of her grief. Perhaps the best assistance he could provide would be to lend her a pair of listening ears. After all these years, it seemed unlikely that she would find those answers.

"Hey! Surprised to see you sitting all alone," Cameron said as he walked up. "I can't think of the last time you didn't have a dining companion," he said, handing Declan a menu.

"I'm meeting my friend Annie for lunch. She should be here any minute," he announced, his lips twitching at the kooky T-shirt Cameron was wearing. It featured a moose drinking coffee.

"The new librarian?" Cameron asked. When Declan nodded, he continued. "Paige said there are already a dozen men or more clamoring to take her out. They said she can't be pried away from the library setup, but once she has some free time, there are plenty of men who are going to try to woo her. Pretty impressive, huh?"

Declan slapped the menu down on the table. "Yep," Declan snapped. "That's the way of things around here lately. The minute a beautiful woman steps foot in town, the buzzards start circling."

Cameron chuckled. "That's a little harsh, isn't it? I mean, this is all Jasper's doing, if you recall. Operation Love was his grand plan. His call to action to save the town." He shook his head. "You can't blame men for wanting to get dibs."

Declan scowled. "Dibs? Annie Murray is the town librarian, Cam. Not a toy to be claimed by some lonesome Alaskan bachelors," he grumbled. He let out a grunt. "Dibs! Never heard of such a thing."

Cameron gaped at him. "That plane crash might have scrambled your brain, Declan. I wasn't saying anything even remotely like that." He placed another menu down across from him. "Why don't I leave you to ponder the menu? We have a new turkey and Swiss wrap with pastrami that folks are going crazy over. I'll throw in two mochaccinos for you and Annie as a way of welcoming her to town. As far as I know, she hasn't been in here yet." Cameron shook his head at him as if he didn't quite know what to make of him.

Declan muttered under his breath as he watched Cameron walk toward the kitchen. Maybe he had been a bit touchy about the subject of Annie. He felt protective of her, which made it hard for him to hear about half the male population in town drooling over her. She was so much more than a participant in Operation Love. Annie had heart and soul and depth. Some of these men knew little or nothing about how to court a woman. Declan laughed out loud. Their idea of a date was moose watching.

Just then he spotted Annie sailing through the door of the café. Once again, she was decked out in an outfit that harkened back to another era. Vintage clothes, if he wasn't mistaken. She was wearing black tights and a black dress with red cherries printed on it. A red wool coat reached down to her knees. Once again, she was wearing her Lovely boots. She looked breathtaking.

He waved her over to his seat, frowning at several

men who attempted to stop Annie from making her way toward him. They were full of smiles and flirtatious gestures. Just as he was about to stand up and escort her over, he watched as she smiled politely, then sidestepped them.

Declan jumped up to pull out Annie's chair for her. A few hostile glares were sent in his direction by some of the male patrons. He couldn't help but grin at them. The looks on their faces made him want to crack up laughing. So much for dibs.

"Good afternoon, Declan," Annie said as she stopped at his table and sat down. "How was your flight to Kodiak this morning?" she asked.

He'd been hoping Annie wouldn't inquire about his client. "Hi, Annie. Unfortunately I didn't make the run," he confessed.

She paused in the process of taking off her coat. Her dark lashes fluttered. "What happened?"

"I had a bad feeling about Ethel not being fit to make the trip. Spent the morning giving her the once-over and a little maintenance," he said lamely. Backing out of a scheduled flight was a new thing for him. Never in all of his years of flying had he done so. And he wasn't feeling good about it. Fear and anxiety had driven the decision, and he hated the way it felt to have done something so uncharacteristic for all the wrong reasons.

"She was fine last week when she flew us back to Love," Annie noted. "Or so it seemed."

"After what happened with Lucy, I had to make sure," he said sheepishly. "At this point, the stakes are too high to make reckless choices."

Annie leaned forward in her chair and put her arms

on the table. "It's okay to be a little reticent about flying again. It's only natural that you would have some jitters after the crash."

"That's not it!" he said with a fierce shake of his head. "I can't risk a plane malfunction. Not when I'm down to one plane," he insisted. He could hear the hard edge to his voice. Why couldn't he just admit to Annie that he was nervous to fly again?

Annie bit her lip. "I don't want to overstep, but you seem…troubled about something."

How in the world could Annie read him so well? He'd been doing his best to keep a lid on his chaotic feelings. Her steady gaze let him know she wasn't going to be pacified if he shrugged off her concern. "I had a rather disappointing conversation with the insurance company," he admitted. He drummed his fingers on the table and looked down. "Because I changed my policy a few months ago, the payout from the insurance company is going to fall short of what I need to buy another plane."

"Oh, Declan," Annie said, her tone infused with empathy. "Is there any way to bridge the gap between the insurance payout and the cost of a seaplane?"

"I have to be honest." He ran his hand over his face as the enormity of the situation crashed over him. "I don't know how I'm going to make up the difference. It's only been recently that we've begun to bring in a steady income and provide a salary for another pilot. Sadly it hasn't allowed me to shore up my savings account."

That was putting it mildly. His savings account was paltry at best. If he thought about it any longer, he wasn't sure he could keep his head up. Everything he had worked so hard to achieve hung in the balance. And it scared him. Who was Declan O'Rourke without his aviation company? All this time he'd been trying to build something for himself, a legacy that would help him stamp out the darkness of his past.

"I wish there was something I could do to help," Annie said. A sad expression was etched on her face. She bowed her head. "I'm going to put my thinking cap on and pray about it. That's what I always do when something seems insurmountable."

He reached across the table and lifted her chin up. "Hey. It's not the end of the world. I'll land on my feet. I always do. Prayers are always appreciated, though," he said in a lighthearted tone.

Never let 'em see you cry. After a lifetime of living by that credo, it was hard to let it go, especially since the thought of being vulnerable in front of Annie terrified him. Even after his mother's death, he had stuffed all those feelings down and buried them. Somewhere along the way, he had learned that showing vulnerability was a weakness.

"Hey, Declan! Sorry that it took me so long to come take y'all's order!" Sophie stood beside their table with two mochaccinos in her hands. She also was wearing the official Moose Café T-shirt with a big-eyed moose on it.

Declan felt an immediate sense of relief when Sophie showed up at the perfect moment. She diffused the heavy tension that had been lingering in the air.

Sophie placed the drinks down on the table. "These are on the house, per Cameron's instructions." She flashed a huge grin in Annie's direction. "Howdy! You must be Annie Murray. I've heard so much about you. I'm Sophie Miller. And believe it or not, we're neighbors at the Black Bear Cabins." She stuck out her hand. Annie reached out and shook it vigorously. I've been meaning to drop in on you at the cabins, but my work schedule has been crazy lately. I've been working the early-morning shift."

"Nice to meet you, Sophie," Annie murmured. "Hazel mentioned we were neighbors. No wonder we haven't crossed paths. Most of my waking hours have been spent over at the library."

"Pleased to meet you. I'd love to catch up with you, Annie, when I have some downtime. I can give you some pointers on life in a small fishing village and how to make a smooth transition to Alaskan living." She looked around at the bustling crowd of diners. "Let me take your order before this place erupts into chaos. What'll it be, folks?"

Annie looked at Declan. "Why don't the two of you suggest something since this is my first time here?" She swung her gaze back up to Sophie. "Any specials?"

"Lots of specials. Today we have a really nice halibut chowder, a Reuben sandwich with polenta fritters, caribou stew in a bread bowl and turkey-lime burgers with sweet potato fries," Sophie recited off the top of her head.

"And there's always reindeer pizza," Declan said. He rubbed his stomach with appreciation.

Annie wrinkled her nose. "I think I'll pass on the reindeer pizza. At least for now," she said.

Sophie winked at her. "It's an acquired taste. If people had told me a year ago that I would enjoy reindeer pizza, I would have called them all kinds of crazy."

"The halibut chowder sounds perfect," Annie said. "I'm starving."

"And I'll have the Reuben sandwich," Declan said, scooping up the menus and handing them to Sophie.

"Coming up in a jiffy," Sophie chirped as she walked away.

Annie's gaze trailed after Sophie. "She's quite the whirlwind."

Declan let out a throaty chuckle. "She's a sweetheart through and through. Not a single mean bone in her entire body. Like yourself, Sophie came to Love to be a participant in Operation Love. She's really found her groove as a barista and waitress here at the café."

"She's like a burst of sunshine," Annie said, her voice filled with awe. "That's priceless."

Declan took a swig of his drink and let out a sigh of appreciation. "Cameron sure does know how to make a mean mochaccino." He placed his drink back down. "So, why don't you tell me about your search? How's it going?"

Annie bit her lip. "I don't want to bend your ear about my quest to find my roots when you're in such a pickle."

A pickle! Yes, he was definitely up a creek without a paddle at the moment. And it scared him. A heavy weight had been sitting on his chest ever since the crash. And after his discussion with the insurance agent, the harsh realities were beginning to set in. He knew far too well that this situation had the potential to derail O'Rourke Charters and rip apart his life in the process.

"You're down to one plane and you're experiencing…" her voice trailed off. She cleared her throat. "Mechanical difficulties?" She raised an eyebrow at him.

"There's nothing I can do about it at the moment. Hearing about your search for your grandfather will serve as a distraction." He jutted his chin in her direction. "Give me something else to think about."

"If you insist." She let out a little sigh and pulled a journal from her purse. She held it up for him to see. "I've studied this inside and out. Gram was a little inconsistent about writing in it every day, but her descriptions are so vivid that I feel like I was right there alongside her. She talks about her friends, life here in Love and falling for a young man she had known since she was a tadpole, as she calls it."

Declan could see the excitement lighting up her face. Once again he was very conscious of how attractive Annie was, particularly when she smiled. It filled him with a sense of happiness to see her so delighted. He sensed that Annie wanted to be tied to people. Having lost her grandmother, she was clearly seeking meaningful connections. Finding her grandfather in Love would give her a sense of being linked to something solid.

He couldn't help but wonder if Annie was being overly optimistic. Was she so blinded by her desire for family ties that she was dreaming of things that might never come to pass?

Declan didn't want to imagine her being disappointed if this all didn't unfold the way she expected. Perhaps it was his job to bring her down to earth and ground her in reality.

He splayed his hands on the wooden table and leaned forward. "So, what's your grand plan, Annie? Where do you see this going from here?"

She blew out a deep breath. Her eyes radiated excitement. "This may sound brash, but I want to tell him that I think I'm his granddaughter."

He knitted his brows together. "Did I miss something? Him who?" Declan asked.

She met his gaze, her brown eyes sparkling with conviction. "The man I've deduced was Gram's one true love. Jasper Prescott, that's who."

Declan began to sputter uncontrollably. He coughed into his hand. He reached for his mochaccino and took a lengthy sip. He plunked the mug back down. "J-Jasper! That's who you think is your long-lost grandfather? The mayor of Love?"

"Yes, I do," Annie said with a determined tilt of her chin. "All the facts point toward him. I've read every word in Gram's journal dozens of times. It all fits together like pieces of a puzzle."

"Annie," Declan said. "Of all the people to set your sights on," he said with a groan.

"It's not like I chose him. Gram did," she said, opening the journal and scanning it for a few moments before placing it in front of Declan. She pointed to the top of a page. "See? Read it. Right there."

Declan peered down at the journal and squinted. "I—I can't make out her cursive writing. Too many loops and curves."

"Let me read it for you," Annie said. With a quick glance around her to make sure no one could overhear, she proceeded to read. "'Spent the day at Nottingham

Woods with the gang. Jasper is such a gentleman.'"
She raised her eyes up from the diary and gave Declan a knowing look.

"What? Is that it? You think Jasper is your grandfather due to some random comment about his manners?" Declan sat back in his chair and folded his arms across his chest. He let out a sigh.

"That's not the only reference," she said in a low voice. "Check this one out." She quickly flipped through the journal "Aha! 'I danced with Jasper cheek to cheek. Swoon.'"

Declan let out a hoot of laughter. "If this were a court of law, your case would be thrown out on its ear."

Annie felt her cheeks reddening. His gibe wounded her. She slammed the journal shut. "I didn't come here to be laughed at! This isn't a joke to me. He might be the only family link I have left in this world."

Declan reached out and grabbed her hand. "I'm sorry. It just struck me as a tad funny. Please tell me there are some guys who show up in that diary other than Jasper."

Annie took out her notebook and peered down at what she had written. She frowned.

"There are others she mentions. Eli, Zach and Killian."

Declan shot up in his chair. "Killian. That's my grandpop."

Annie began writing furiously in her notebook. By the time she swung her gaze back up, the expression on Declan's face had shifted to one of mild panic. "What's the matter?" She threw her head back and laughed. "I hope you don't think we're related."

Declan gulped. "Well, you did throw his name out there."

"In these pages, Gram makes it clear that Killian was married to her best friend, Lucy. Sounds like they got married at an early age. High school, I believe."

Declan let out the breath he'd been holding. "Yes. My grandparents were very devoted to each other until the day she died."

"Lucy!" Annie said in an awed voice. "You named your plane after her."

"I did," Declan acknowledged with a nod. "She was pure sweetness, my grandmother. Way too fragile for the Alaskan lifestyle."

"Did she leave as part of the exodus Jasper mentioned in his interview?" Annie asked. She knew from reading newspaper interviews featuring Jasper that his own wife, Harmony, had been one of the many women to have picked up stakes and left Love for greener pastures. The exodus from Love decades ago had led to the male-female imbalance in the present that had caused Jasper to create the Operation Love program.

"No, she didn't. A lot of her best friends and relatives left, but she remained stalwart. She stuck it out in Alaska until she passed on to glory, Annie. Truly I think that's the only thing that could have separated her from Grandpop."

Nothing but love emanated from Declan's voice. And deep respect. Although she was tempted to ask about his parents, she knew better than to open a can of worms. She didn't want to bring up a topic that might cause him pain. Hazel's words rang in her ears. *Finn and Declan lost their childhood, all in one fell swoop.* It was reassuring to know that despite the tragedies that had marred his young life, there had been other influences at play. His grandparents had demonstrated the enduring nature of their love.

"That's a blessing. To know that your grandparents shared such an amazing love story must make you proud."

He nodded, then cleared his throat. "I was extremely fortunate to have them."

Sophie suddenly reappeared with a tray bursting with the smell of delicious dishes. She expertly held the tray on her hip as she lowered the plates to the table. Annie let out exclamation of delight as the aroma of the halibut chowder filled her nostrils. A piece of corn bread sat on a separate plate. Her stomach started doing somersaults at the sight of the food.

"Enjoy! Let me know if you need anything else," Sophie said with a wave.

For the next few minutes, they ate in companionable silence. Annie wasn't sure why, but she felt as comfortable with Declan as she had with her old friends back home. Was it possible that near tragedy had forced them to bond more rapidly than normal? Or was there something about Declan that was innately special? Were her feelings for him strictly friendship, or was there something more going on?

Annie pushed her bowl away from her after emptying it of fish chowder. "That was terrific," she gushed. "It was the perfect blend of ingredients and spices."

Declan stuffed the last morsel of sandwich in his mouth. He picked up his napkin and wiped his lips. "Not sure how we survived without this place," he said. "So, Annie, how can I help you figure this whole thing out?"

"I'm going to be very strategic and line up all my ducks in a row. Once I compile enough evidence to make a strong case, I'm going to confront Jasper and get some answers."

Declan sent her a somber look. "Remember, Annie, a lot of water has flowed under that bridge. Your grandmother left Alaska decades ago. You're going to have to bring forward compelling evidence to sway Jasper Prescott. And if I were you, I'd make sure that the evidence points toward him before you single him out."

He was right. The last thing she needed to do was alienate the town mayor. So far she was really loving her job at the library. In the weeks and months ahead, she was going to need Jasper to support fund-raising initiatives and programs. There were already many events on the calendar that Jasper and the town council had green-lighted, such as the winter-wonderland event at Deer Run Lake.

"Since you asked how you can be of service, I'd like you to take a look at Gram's notations. I know you said her writing was swirly, but once you read a little bit of it, you'll get used to it. This way, I can have another set of eyes giving it the once-over." She waited with bated breath for Declan to answer. Annie didn't want to beg him, but she needed someone else's opinion about Gram's entries.

"All right," he said after a few moments. "I'll read it. That's all I'm promising right now. I'll give it the once-over and see if I can pick up on any clues."

She reached into her bag for the diary and slid it across the table. Declan blew out a huff of air when he saw it. With a look of reluctance etched on his face, he picked it up and studied the small leather-bound book. "I really hope this isn't going to turn into something out of one of those crazy paternity shows. 'You are not the grandfather,'" he said with a rueful shake of his head.

"Of course it won't," Annie said, her lips twitching in amusement at Declan's comment. "I want this whole matter to be handled with the utmost dignity. My goal is to find my family, but I don't want to hurt anyone in the process. I can't pretend that I don't want answers, but deep down I'm hoping I find a family that embraces me."

Declan let out what sounded like a sigh of relief. She couldn't put her finger on it, but she sensed he was troubled about her plan of action. Was he concerned about her creating a scandal in the small fishing village?

She pushed her chair back and placed some bills down on the table. "I really have to be getting back to the library," she said. "My lunch hour is almost up."

Declan reached for the bills and pushed them back toward her. He stood up from his seat. "It's my treat. You can take me out to lunch next time," he said with a pearly grin.

Next time? She felt a lurching sensation inside her stomach. The last thing she wanted to do was to start looking forward to these shared moments with Declan. He bordered on being irresistible with his magnetic smile, his comedic flair and the vibe of goodness he radiated. It was dangerous for her to be lulled into thinking he was marriage material. He'd even admitted from his own lips that he wasn't the settling-down type. And she'd seen with her own eyes the way he flirted with the single ladies in town. It would be a huge mistake to convince herself that she could change his mind. Many women had broken their own hearts by believing they could inspire a man to want marriage and the whole nine yards.

He was her friend, she reassured herself. One who had saved her life and was helping her with a search that was near and dear to her heart. Any romantic feelings she might harbor toward him needed to be stuffed down into the inner labyrinths of her heart.

With a grateful smile, Annie placed the bills back in her purse. Before she knew what was happening, Declan was at her side, helping her on with her coat. Once she had both arms in the sleeves, he helped her button it up so that her throat wasn't exposed. As his knuckles grazed her neck, she felt a frisson of awareness pass between them. Declan's eyes widened, letting her know he'd felt the same jolt of electricity.

The gentlemanly gesture left her breathless. With a shaky wave of her hand, she turned on her booted heel and walked toward the exit of the Moose Café. On her way out, several gentlemen tried to stop her for a bit of conversation. All she did was smile politely and keep moving. Hazel had warned her about the large number of bachelors, who could be overzealous at times in their pursuit of the single women in town. She felt a twinge of guilt that she didn't have the slightest interest in a single one of them.

Little did they know, but after she'd crash-landed with Declan O'Rourke, these men had a hard act to follow. Near impossible, she mused.

She began to hum a happy tune as she strolled down Jarvis Street toward the Free Library of Love. Right across the street from the Moose Café, she noticed a sign for the sheriff's office. The quaint little shops caused her to pause and look in their windows. She peered in the window of an old-fashioned barbershop and watched as a man had his beard shaved off. When she passed by a little bookstore, The Bookworm, she started thinking about how the store and the library could help each other and cross-promote the value of reading a good book. She increased her pace as the wind started to whip up and a few snowflakes began to swirl all around her. The sky was turning a pewter shade. Annie burrowed into her coat as a refuge from the wind and cold.

All of her goals were being accomplished, one by one. Coming all the way to Love, Alaska, had been the big goal. She had begun her job as librarian and was now working with local officials on shoring up money to restore full-time hours to the library. Her quest to find her grandfather was gaining steam. A thrill coursed through her at the idea that in mere weeks, she might have a family to belong to. Everything was falling into place just as she had imagined. Putting her foot in the dating pool and finding a husband would make her joy complete.

Now if she could somehow manage to stop her heart from soaring every time Declan was in her presence, everything in her new Alaskan life would be perfect.

Chapter Eight

Over the next few days, Declan found himself entertained by the journal entries of Aurelia Alice Murray. Through the pages of her diary, she had come vividly to life for him. She came across as witty, spunky and adventurous. Her circle of friends had been tight-knit and congenial. And he had to admit that her admiration of Jasper shone through the pages like a beacon. Alice had portrayed him as a knight in shining armor. He wished he could share the journal with Boone, who would surely get a hearty laugh out of that one! He chuckled as an image floated in his mind of Jasper dressed up like a knight from medieval times. Declan laughed so hard he had to put the journal down in order to wipe away tears of mirth.

As the entries continued, Declan sensed a less than lighthearted tone. Alice hinted at conflicts within the group and worries that kept her up late at night. He wondered if her turmoil coincided with her discovery that she was expecting a child. There were comments about her unsupportive parents and wanting to run far away from her small town. Declan also had the feeling that she was editing herself and leaving out huge chunks of information. Otherwise, why was there no discussion of her pregnancy or the father of her child?

Declan had woken up this morning with an agenda. Ever since the plane crash, Willard had agreed to do the runs until he was ready to go up in the air again. Although Declan hadn't fully explained his reasons for not doing the gigs himself, Willard was eager to keep a steady paycheck and to get his flying hours in. Since they were down to only one plane, he'd been forced to adjust a few of O'Rourke Charter's clients and cancel some gigs.

His first stop was going to be the library. He'd placed a book on reserve about the history of aviation in the United States. The book had been on order, according to Annie, but hadn't yet arrived at the library. A message left on his voice mail had alerted him to the fact that the book was now ready to be picked up. He also wanted to ask Annie if she would like to go with him to the winter-wonderland event being held at Deer Run Lake. There would be ice-skating and tobogganing and plenty of Alaskan fun to be had by all. It wouldn't be a date. More like friends hanging out together.

And even though he knew nothing serious could ever develop between him and Annie, he couldn't deny that he wanted to spend some time with her in a festive atmosphere. They were friends, after all, weren't they?

He didn't want to pat himself on the back, but he'd stepped up to help the committee organize the event. It didn't sit well with him that he had initially lobbied against library funds. Although the inevitable budget issues with regard to the library had nothing to do with his actions, he still wanted to help bolster the funding. After seeing the huge impact libraries had on communities, he felt like a killjoy for being on the opposite side of it.

The moment he stepped inside the library walls, Declan felt a sense of peace wash over him. The library felt so cozy. Everything was stilled and hushed. It had a nice vibe. Everywhere he looked he saw small children with their mothers. He nodded to a few people he knew and waved at their children. When he finally found Annie at the circulation desk, talking to Dwight, he almost did a double take.

What was Dwight doing here? He looked like a puppy dog, the way he was practically salivating over Annie. Declan stood at a distance, obscured by one of the tall columns. He watched as Dwight reached for Annie's hand and shook it. Declan rolled his eyes. If this was Dwight's version of courting Annie, he seriously needed to step up his game. He shook his head as he watched Dwight walk away with a goofy grin on his face. A wave of jealousy roared through him. Ugh. He hated feeling this way, especially since he knew he had no claim on Annie.

Annie was facing in the other direction as he crept up to her.

"Oh, Miss Librarian. Can you help me find a book?" he asked in a singsong voice.

Annie whirled around. Her face lit up with a smile when she saw it was him standing there. "Declan! What brings you here? Are you on the hunt for a good book?"

"I'm actually picking one up," he said, a tinge of

pride evident in his tone. "I reserved it a few days ago."

She snapped her fingers. "Oh, that's right. The aviation book that we'd placed on order. Let me find it for you," she offered as she began walking toward a cart loaded with books. He followed behind her, marveling at how smoothly things appeared to be running at the library. Annie had a confident air, one that hinted at a great wealth of knowledge. She perused the books and pulled one out that had his last name taped to the side. Annie paused a moment to look at it before handing it to him. "Good stuff, O'Rourke. This should be fascinating reading."

He nodded, feeling pleased at his selection. "I'm not a big reader, but if I find an interesting topic, I can't put the book down."

Annie's grin threatened to split her face wide-open. "That's the exact feeling I want readers to have when they start a great book."

He shifted from one foot to the other. Suddenly he felt nervous about asking Annie if she wanted to go to the fund-raiser. Would she think it was a date? Or would it simply be two friends hanging out at a town event? Truth be told, he wasn't sure if he knew the answer to that himself. The longer this stretched out, the more conflicted he felt about it.

"Hey, Annie. I was wondering if you wanted to come to the winter-wonderland event with me." He grinned at her. "I promise it will be a lot of fun."

Her face fell. She bit her lip. "Oh, Declan, I would have loved to go with you, but Dwight just asked me a few minutes ago to be his date. And I said yes."

Dwight? Annie and Dwight were going to the

event together? And here he'd just been snickering about Dwight's lack of finesse. At the moment, the joke was on him. The town treasurer had just swept in and asked Annie to the fund-raiser. He felt his face getting heated. Just the thought of the two of them together made him feel out of sorts.

"That's okay," he said in a casual tone. "I'm sure the two of you will have lots of fun." He was trying his best to keep any hint of sarcasm out of his voice. Having a good time with Dwight seemed near impossible as far as he was concerned. He was about as entertaining as a wet blanket.

"I'm sure there are dozens of women in the Operation Love program who would love to go with you," Annie said. "From what I hear and from what I've seen with my own eyes, they practically have a Declan O'Rourke fan club going on."

He knew Annie's statement was somewhat true—ladies in town wanted to date him. He had taken quite a few of the Operation Love ladies out on dates over the past few months or so. However, there was no fan club. Not that he knew of, anyway. So far, a few ladies had laid down some heavy hints about attending the event with him. The problem was, there wasn't a single one of them he wanted to ask except Annie. And thanks to Dwight, she was taken.

No one could make him laugh the way Annie could. No one made him think like she did, either. There was always something interesting she brought to the table. Some rare fact he had no clue about. She seemed to enjoy his sense of humor, and he loved seeing his hometown through her eyes. Everything in Love was so new to Annie, and she seemed to be getting the most out of every moment of her journey.

"Have you read Gram's journal?" she asked. "I've been dying for your verdict."

"I read a little bit," he hedged. "I want to wait till I finish the whole diary to give you my assessment." The more he read of the diary, the more he was becoming uncomfortable about Jasper's possible link to Annie.

"That's fine," she said. "I know you have a lot on your plate these days. Have you heard from the FAA?"

"Not yet. It should be any day now, though," he said. "A lot is riding on this for me."

"I know, Declan," she said in a mournful tone. "I'm offering up prayers on your behalf. You're a fantastic pilot. I know the investigation will clear you."

"Thanks, Annie," he said, wishing he could rely on prayer alone.

"Have a good day." With a simple wave, he walked away from her, his thoughts tied up in the fate of O'Rourke Charters and the plane crash.

His stomach had been in knots for days in anticipation of the findings. He'd sent up more prayers to the big guy upstairs than he cared to count. Although he knew God was in his corner, he had a hard time feeling worthy of all his prayers being answered. What was so special about Declan O'Rourke that he should be so blessed? He'd learned early in life that bad things happened to people, and prayers didn't stop them from happening. When his mother had died so suddenly, it had felt as if the sun had been stamped out of the sky. And despite his suffering, the wheels of life had continued to spin.

If the worst happened and the accident was deemed pilot error, he would be devastated. It would be a huge blow to his career and self-confidence. But the world would keep turning on its axis, and he would pick himself up, dust himself off and move forward.

It's what he had always done. This time would be no different.

Annie let out a sigh as Declan sailed out the door of the library. She admired the way he walked. The strong tilt of his head belied the anxiety she sensed was riding under the surface. Although he presented a good picture of someone who was holding everything together, Annie feared he wasn't doing well at all. She had it on good authority from Hazel that Declan hadn't flown Ethel yet on any of the client runs. His employee, Willard, had filled in for him each and every time, which meant that Declan was still avoiding flying his seaplane.

The very idea of Declan struggling to find his way in the aftermath of the plane crash caused her stomach to tighten painfully. Annie didn't want to see him hurting. She cared about him way more than she wanted to admit, even to herself.

Lord, please watch over Declan. Lift him up and restore his confidence. I don't think he realizes how important he is to this town. Or what a good man he truly is.

It had gutted her to have to say no to his invitation to be his date to the fund-raiser event. Talk about bad timing! If he had arrived a few minutes earlier, Declan would have beaten Dwight to the punch. Poor Dwight.

He seemed like the type of man who was looking for some companionship.

The sight of an older, silver-haired gentleman entering the library caused her to sit up straight in her chair. There were two other men walking behind him at a much slower pace. Within seconds she had identified the man in front as Mayor Prescott. He was striding toward her with a look of purpose etched on his handsome face.

Jasper Prescott! Just being in proximity to him made her pulse race with exhilaration. This man could be her grandfather. He was distinguished and stately and, by all accounts, a barrel of fun. And he had an extensive family and enough relatives to give her a plethora of familial connections right here in Love. She knew that she was getting ahead of herself, but she was hoping and wishing and praying that he was her long-lost kin.

"Good morning, Annie. I brought some pals along with me. These boys have been lifelong friends of mine. We were as thick as thieves growing up," he said with a wink. "This is Eli Courtland, and this is Zachariah Cummings."

"It's great to see you again, Mayor Prescott," she gushed. There was something about the man that was infectious. It didn't take a genius to see why Hazel was so enamored of him.

"Nice to meet you, Annie," Eli said as he reached for her hand and shook it. "Thanks for bringing all your knowledge about books to our little town."

Annie turned toward Zachariah, who studied her with a wary expression. He barely grunted a hello.

"Don't mind him," Jasper said in a loud whisper

as he leaned in to her. "He got up on the wrong side of the bed this morning."

"Just this morning?" Eli asked with a guffaw.

"I've been itching to show off our new library, since they both missed the ribbon-cutting ceremony," Jasper explained.

"Cilla was home with a bad cold," Eli said. "I didn't have the heart to leave her alone."

Cilla. The name immediately drew Annie's attention. Gram had written about her. She had been one of her closest friends.

Jasper clapped Eli on the back. "Can't say as I blame you. That's what makes you such a great husband, Eli. You're as devoted as they come."

Annie thought she heard a snort from Zachariah.

"Welcome to the Free Library of Love, gentlemen. Is there anything I can help you find in our catalog? Or are you just getting the grand tour?" Annie asked. It was incredibly sweet that Jasper had brought his two dearest friends to get a glimpse of Love's new and improved library. It was wonderful that the town mayor was as proud of it as she was.

"Let's start with a tour of the place," Jasper suggested. "Then I'd love to find a few of my favorite authors in the catalog."

"I wish that I was a more proficient reader like Jasper here," Eli said mournfully as he looked all around him. There was a wistful expression in his eyes. "I would love to take some books out and get a library card with my name on it."

"Me, too," Zachariah said with a frown.

"Both of you are eligible for a library card," Annie

informed them. "Even if you're not strong readers, you can still fill out the form and get your own card."

"Oh, Annie, that's great. I'd love to bring some books home for my wife," Eli said, his face lit up with happiness. "Cilla loves to read."

Zachariah still seemed caught up in the past. "Back in our day, if you fell behind, the teacher didn't have the time or the resources to help you catch up."

"That's true," Eli asserted. "So we just limped along."

"And ended up being pitiful readers," Zachariah said with a rueful shake of his head.

"But not for lack of trying," Eli said with a little sigh. "We really wanted to excel at it."

Annie turned toward Jasper and discreetly pulled him aside while the other two men continued their discussion. "Maybe we can have some literacy programs for adults at the library. It could help strengthen skills and foster a love of books. And it might provide some incentive to add some more hours to the schedule."

"It's a good idea," Jasper said. "I just wonder if folks in town would be too proud to come seeking help."

"There's nothing to be ashamed of. Plenty of adults struggle with reading and don't become fully functional readers till later on in life."

Jasper reached for her hand. "I like the way you think, Annie. Let's make it happen. If you can do a little research and draft a proposal, I'll have the town council discuss it. We do have a special fund for education that we might be able to tap into."

"Excellent. I'll get right on it. Shall we tour the library?" Annie asked.

Jasper held out his arm and waited for Annie to loop her arm through his. "Lead the way, milady," he said with a nod of his head. "We can't wait to see all the progress you and your team have made."

"We're still getting things settled, but during the days the library is closed—Fridays and weekends— we'll be putting on the finishing touches," Annie said.

As Annie walked arm in arm with Jasper, trailed by Eli and Zachariah, she felt a burst of pride in this wonderful, charming place. A library was a treasured building, filled with books and educational materials that could transform lives. If she lived to be one hundred, she didn't think she would ever forget the look of awe on Eli's and Zachariah's faces as they went from room to room. She couldn't help but wonder if their own lives might have been different if there had been a fully functioning library in this town when they were growing up. By her calculations, they had been adults when the first library had opened in town. Sadly the library had closed its doors after only a few short years due to financial issues and lack of interest from the townsfolk.

The enormity of it washed over her. In traveling all the way to Love, she had been determined to see this library make a difference in the residents' lives. And little by little, she was discovering that her presence here in town really could make an impact.

Yes, indeed. She was exactly where she needed to be.

Chapter Nine

It was a perfect night for a toboggan ride, Declan thought. A crisp chill permeated the air. A full moon hung in the sky. There was ample snow on the ground to make the toboggans glide like lightning down the hill. A few delicate snowflakes gently fell from the heavens. As he looked out over Deer Run Lake, he inhaled deeply. The fresh Alaskan air felt invigorating. The frozen-solid lake appeared as smooth as glass. He let out a chuckle as he flashed back to all the memorable times he'd spent in this very place with Finn and the Prescott brothers.

Declan was floating on air. A few hours ago, he had received a phone call from the FAA informing him that the accident had occurred due to a bird strike. In his specific case, birds had been sucked into an engine, striking an engine fan blade. As a result, Lucy had gone down.

He felt vindicated! Even though no one had blamed him for the plane crash, he'd placed the responsibility on his own shoulders as the pilot. Now, for the first time in weeks, he could rid himself of the albatross he'd been carrying around his neck.

A bird strike! Of all the things to force him to make a crash landing. He could hardly believe it. He hadn't seen any birds that morning when they'd left Anchorage, although there had been a light fog in the area. Perhaps that explained why he hadn't noticed any flying near the plane.

It was neither here nor there. He was celebrating his good news and feeling hopeful that this nightmare was coming to an end.

All he wanted to do was find Annie and grab her by the hand so he could tell her the good news. It was a pretty novel feeling for him—this desire to share life-changing news with a woman. He'd never had that relationship with anyone before. Declan hadn't wanted that type of closeness. If he was being honest with himself, he'd resisted it at every turn. And of all the women to inspire this feeling inside him, Annie was the one woman who wanted the things he couldn't provide.

The smell of apple cider hovered in the air. He could almost taste it going down his throat, warm and spicy. Declan found himself wishing he had hustled up a date for this evening. Everywhere he looked, couples were huddled together or standing in line at the concession stand, holding hands. Almost as if he had made her appear by thinking about her, Annie came into view. She was standing by the concession stand, too, her pretty face framed by a dark pair of earmuffs. As soon as she spotted him, Annie waved at him enthusiastically.

He wasn't the jealous type, but the sight of Dwight

with Annie by his side threatened to drive him crazy. His insides twisted painfully. Not that he had any claim on her or anything! But seeing her with Dwight, of all people, was grating on his nerves. Dwight! He was the most humorless, negative person on the planet, while Annie was cheery and good-hearted.

This feeling brewing inside him felt like torture.

Humph! It served him right. He should have been quicker about asking her to the event himself, even though he had no intention of dating Annie. But they could have gone as friends. Surely there was no harm in that.

Who was he kidding? What he felt for Annie wasn't strictly friendship. He wasn't sure what he wanted, and his feelings were becoming more complicated each and every day. All he knew was that it scared him all the way down to his toes.

"Hey, Declan," Cameron called out, motioning him over to the roasting fire. He was sitting with his beautiful wife, Paige, and their baby daughter, Emma, roasting marshmallows. Declan moved toward them, thankful for a distraction from the sight of Annie coupled up with Dwight. There was only so much of it he could stand before he exploded.

"How are you?" Paige asked, standing up to give him a hug. "I haven't seen you since the accident. It goes without saying that we were mighty happy to know you made it through the ordeal unscathed."

All of a sudden, Boone's voice intruded on the conversation, and he felt a strong pat on his back. "It would take more than a plane crash to take this guy down," Boone drawled. "He's as solid as they come."

"You got that right," Declan said, enjoying being

in the bosom of the Prescott family. "Where's your better half?" Declan teased, looking past Boone for any signs of Grace.

"Gracie sends her regards," Boone said, his expression downcast. "She's beat. This little one is really wearing her mother out. Between exhaustion and battling morning sickness, Gracie is having a tough time of it." Boone's expression exuded concern.

"Poor thing. I know it's tough, but she'll be all right. She doesn't have too much longer to go," Paige said. "Trust me. It'll all be worth it in the end." She sat back down and pressed a kiss on her daughter's forehead. Cameron gazed at his family, his face practically glowing with contentment. Declan was happy for him. He and Paige had gone through the fire before emerging stronger and more committed to one another than ever.

Emma stood up and pointed to a spot in the distance. "Dan. Dan." She was jumping up and down with excitement. Within seconds her cousin Aidan came into view, accompanied by Liam and Honor, youngest of the Prescott children and sister of Boone, Liam and Cameron.

"She can't say Aidan yet," Cameron explained with a chuckle. "She's been calling him Dan for weeks."

Everyone laughed and enjoyed the sight of Aidan greeting his baby cousin with a sweet hug and a kiss on the cheek. The two children represented the future of the Prescott clan.

"Seems like we have another charmer in our midst," Honor joked. "He's going to give Declan a run for his money."

Declan chuckled along with everyone else, but he

felt a niggling sensation at the idea of being viewed as a ladies' man. More and more he was pushing against the very idea of it. He wasn't sure it was who he wanted to be. Frankly it was getting old.

And the truth of it was, the only woman he wanted to spend time with was Annie. *Sweet, beautiful Annie.* She was intelligent and caring and interesting beyond belief. He could talk to her for hours without being bored. And if he had to be stranded alone with anyone on a desert island, he'd pick her.

"Now, this is a sight for sore eyes!" a raspy voice rang out. Jasper, bundled up in a fur-trimmed parka, walked up with Hazel at his side. Declan couldn't help but smile at the rapturous look on Hazel's face. She really did love the old coot. He hoped Jasper appreciated Hazel's devotion. "I love seeing this family as one big, tight unit." He swung his gaze around the circle. "We've weathered some rough times, but from this point forward it's smooth sailing."

Declan knew with a deep certainty that Jasper was referencing his own health issues, the loss of Liam's beloved wife, Ruby, and the town of Love's recession. Not to mention Boone's estrangement with his sister, Honor, and Cameron having missed the first fourteen months of his daughter's life. The Prescott family had been through the ringer over the past few years.

"Amen!" Hazel said in a loud voice. She raised her hand in the air. "Let the blessings continue for this family."

His family. Declan cast a glance around at all the people who couldn't have been more dear to him if they had been blood relations. His mind suddenly veered toward Finn. At some point, he needed to patch things up with his brother. Although things always tended to be hit or miss with them, he loved Finn. Life was too short not to bridge the gap between them.

"Who wants to ice-skate?" Declan asked, holding his skates up in the air.

Boone let out a groan while Aidan started hollering with excitement. Liam sent Declan a helpless look. It didn't take a genius to figure out what was bothering Liam. He'd seen this all play out before during the last skating party.

"Will you skate with me, Aidan? I came here without a date tonight, so you'd be doing me a big favor."

Aidan turned toward his father. He looked up at him with solemn brown eyes. "Daddy. Do you mind if I skate with Declan?"

Liam lovingly tousled his son's cap of brown curls. "Not at all, buddy. It sounds like fun. Have a great time!"

Liam mouthed the words *thank you* to Declan when his son wasn't looking. It was a well-known fact that none of the three Prescott brothers could skate a lick, which was pretty hilarious considering that learning to ice-skate in Alaska was a rite of passage. Declan didn't mind one bit filling in for Liam. Spending time with Aidan was priceless. With his dark hair, olive skin and expressive eyes, he almost made Declan yearn for a kid of his own.

"Come on A-man," Declan said, using the nickname Boone had given his nephew. Aidan quickly left his father's side and joined Declan. He sat Aidan down and began to lace up his brown ice skates. As soon as he placed his own skates on his feet, he began to lead Aidan onto the ice. Aidan's movements were tentative. Although he knew how to skate a little bit, Declan realized he had a way to go before he could skate around the lake by himself.

A glint of pink whipping around the lake suddenly caught his eye. It was Annie, spectacularly decked out in a pink parka jacket, black leggings and a pair of winter-white ice skates. She came to a stop right next to them, gifting him with a dazzling smile.

He looked around the skating area. "Where's Dwight?" Declan asked with a scowl.

"He can't skate," Annie said with a shrug. "I was so excited about skating here tonight, so he insisted I head out to the ice without him."

"How considerate of him," Declan said, trying to keep his tone neutral. As if he wasn't annoyed enough by Dwight being Annie's date, now he'd just discovered that he didn't even know how to skate. *Count to ten*, he reminded himself. It wasn't fair to take out all his frustrations on Dwight.

"Mind if I join you?" Annie asked. "I can help with Aidan if you like."

Declan nodded. He couldn't think of anything he would like better than to glide around the lake with Annie. It would restore his good mood. From the looks of it, she was a really good skater. Growing up in Maine had probably helped her hone those skills.

"Hey! I don't need help!" Aidan protested. "I'm a big boy."

Annie and Declan shared an amused glance. Declan bent down so that he was on eye level with Aidan. "You really are a big boy, Aidan. I can't believe you're going to be five on your next birthday. But here's the thing." He lowered his voice to a whisper. "Annie isn't the best skater in the world. So we're going to hold hands with her so she doesn't fall."

"Are we going to be heroes?" Aidan asked.

"Yes, we are," Declan said with a nod.

"Daddy says my mommy was a hero. She saved lots of lives," Aidan said. "And now she's in heaven."

Declan placed his arms around Aidan. "She was a true-blue hero, buddy. She was one of the bravest people I've ever known." He placed his hand over his chest as a sharp pain stabbed him. All of sudden, he was catapulted back to his own loss of his beloved mother. The ache never really faded.

It didn't escape his notice that Annie brushed a tear away from her cheek, clearly moved by Aidan's poignant words about his mother.

Aidan nodded solemnly, then glanced over at Annie. He stuck out his hand. "Grab ahold of me. You won't fall. It's not scary at all." Annie took his hand and hung on tightly. Declan skated to the other side of Aidan and grabbed his hand. As a threesome, they began to glide across the lake. The sound of Aidan's carefree laughter carried with the wintry breeze. He glanced over at Annie and locked gazes with her. She smiled at him—a beatific, dazzling smile that caused his pulse to race at ten times its normal pace.

For a man who hadn't had a lot of perfect in his life, Declan relished this carefree, lighthearted moment. It was sheer perfection. All of his troubles seemed to have been swept away by the gusty Alaskan wind. Declan wished this interlude could last forever. Gliding around Deer Run Lake with Annie and Aidan gave him the feeling of soaring, and it was almost as if he had his wings back.

Moved by immense joy, he uttered a prayer of gratitude. *Thank You, Lord, for giving me this moment of pure happiness.*

Annie felt a stab of guilt at how much enjoyment it had given her to skate around the lake with Aidan and Declan by her side. After all, Dwight was her date, not Declan. Aidan was such a little sweetheart. She ached to think of him losing his mother at such a tender age. She knew what it felt like to walk through life without a mother by her side. But she'd always had Gram as a surrogate mother to fill the void. Having met Liam at the opening of the library, she felt certain that he would shepherd his son through life with compassion, hope and an abundance of love.

And Declan. Funny, brave Declan. He was turning out to be so much more than she'd ever imagined. When she had first met him, Declan's handsome face had bowled her over. She had instantly assumed he was nothing more than Alaskan eye candy. How wrong she'd been. There was so much more he had to offer. Personality. Wisdom. Courage. She let out a sigh. Despite her best efforts, she was falling for the gorgeous pilot. Tumbling headlong for the very type of man she'd hoped to avoid—one who didn't want to settle down. One who seemed to embrace his bachelor status.

Dwight had rushed to her side as soon as she'd left the ice. He'd taken her over to the concession stand for hot chocolate and cider donuts. Annie had felt the first stirrings of jealousy when she'd spotted Declan standing with a group of women. His head was thrown back in laughter, and he appeared to be the life of the party.

"Annie? Annie?" Dwight's voice crashed over her, causing her to realize she'd zoned out and was staring at Declan and his entourage.

She turned toward Dwight, who was eyeing her with suspicion. "Is something wrong, Annie? You look a little out of sorts."

"N-no, Dwight. I'm fine," she said, rubbing her mittened hands together. "Just a little nippy out here. The wind is really kicking up."

"We might just see the northern lights tonight if we're fortunate," Dwight said.

Annie tried to smile, but all she could think about was the fact that she wanted to watch the northern lights with Declan by her side. Dwight was nothing more than a friend, while Declan made her heart pitter-patter. And there was nothing more painful than standing here with another man while she was being hit with the realization that she was falling head over heels for Declan. It almost took her breath away, this feeling that hit her like a punch in the gut.

There was no sense pining away for Declan. He wasn't the type who would embrace the idea of settling down. She needed to focus on men who wanted the same things in life as she did. A solid man like Dwight! She didn't feel any romantic sparks with Dwight, but she knew that her focus should be on men like him.

"Have you ever been on a toboggan?" Dwight asked, his eyes radiating enthusiasm.

"Sure. A few times here and there when I was a kid," she said, injecting her voice with eagerness. She didn't want to hurt Dwight's feelings or make him think she'd checked out of their date.

"A few people are going up to Cupid's Hill to sled. Wanna join them?"

Annie looked over at the hill. She could see a group of people careening down the slope on their sleds. It looked like a lot of fun. And Dwight had such an expectant look on his face. There was absolutely no shot of them becoming romantically involved, so she felt obligated to show Dwight that at least she was a good sport.

"Okay," she said with a tight smile. "Let's do it."

By the time Annie had made her way to the top of the hill, she felt winded. From way up on top of Cupid's Hill, it was a long way to the bottom. She was starting to feel nervous. It had been a long time since she'd ridden one of these things.

"We can just grab one of these sleds. Everyone ends up sharing anyway," Dwight explained. He picked out two big toboggans and dragged them over to the top of the run.

"Dwight, I'm not sure I want to do this," she said, biting her lip. "We're really high up here. I'm not exactly the sporty type."

Dwight put his arm around her. "It just looks intimidating, Annie. Trust me. We've been tobogganing down this hill since we were little kids."

Annie peered down the hill. It was a pretty steep incline. She shook her head. "I'm walking back down. I'm sorry to be a killjoy, Dwight, but I'm a little nervous."

"Hey. Why don't we go down together? I'll steer us, okay?"

Annie nodded. Dwight held the toboggan and ushered her to sit down. Annie placed her feet firmly on the snow and straddled the sled, then gingerly sat down. She took another look at the steep incline. It was enough to make her dizzy. *Calm down*, a little voice buzzed in her head. *Live courageously.* Wasn't that her motto for her new life in Alaska?

Just as she caught a glimpse of Dwight positioning himself next to the toboggan, she felt a shift in the sled's position. She let out a cry as the toboggan began to slide down the hill without Dwight on it. With his guttural screams ringing in her ears, Annie held on for dear life as the toboggan careened down the hill at breakneck speed. With no way of stopping the runaway sled and her heart firmly lodged in her throat, all Annie could do was pray to make it out of this without breaking every bone in her body.

Declan sat at the bottom of Cupid's Hill, looking out at Deer Run Lake. There was a tranquility about this place that settled over him like a warm blanket. It was his favorite location in town for that very reason. Everything seemed clearer out here. He could think without the doubts creeping in. Life seemed way simpler when he was standing here, bathed in moonlight and staring up at a star-filled sky.

He turned toward the hill, chuckling as he watched a group of teenagers come to a stop mere seconds before they would have skidded onto the lake. They triumphantly gave each other high fives. Sledding on Cupid's Hill was tricky due to the steep slope of the hill and the way a smattering of trees intersected the route. People who didn't know what they were doing might break their necks by crashing into the copse of trees at the bottom of the hill. Declan had seen quite a few terrible accidents over the years.

"I think someone might be in trouble," one of the teens said, pointing toward the slope.

He followed the boy's gaze and saw the flash of pink, accompanied by the sound of feminine screams as the sled came careening down the hill. Annie! He could see her brown hair flying wildly around her face and the earmuffs covering her ears. One quick glance revealed that she wasn't even attempting to control the toboggan. She was going way too fast and heading directly toward the trees. Declan ran toward her path and veered to the right. With a wild cry he lunged for the reins, using all his weight to jerk the sled toward him. As if in slow motion, he saw Annie roll off the sled and land facedown in the snow.

"Annie!" he yelled, letting go of the reins and scrambling to get to her. When he reached the spot where she lay motionless, he heard her moan softly. "Are you all right?" he asked, gently turning her on her side. Her earmuffs were askew, and snow and ice particles clung to her face.

After a few moments, her eyes fluttered open. "Declan!" she whispered. "You saved me. Again."

Declan blew out a deep breath. "You scared me half to death, Annie. What in the world did you think you were doing, coming down that slope like a runaway train?" He frowned at her. "You could have broken your neck."

Annie struggled to sit up. He steadied her by her arms until she got her bearings. Without any kind of warning, she threw her arms around him and clung to him as if he was a life preserver. He could feel the rapid ins and outs of her breathing through her parka. She was mumbling something that he couldn't quite decipher.

All he knew was that he didn't want to let Annie go. It felt so right to be holding her in his arms and giving her a soft place to fall.

Chapter Ten

Talk about a thrill ride! Annie could still feel her pulse racing like crazy from her dramatic ride down Cupid's Hill. Declan coming to her rescue would go down in her memory as one of the most exciting and heartwarming moments of her life. It had been swoon worthy! Just as she had thought all hope was lost of being able to maneuver herself out of harm's way, he had swept in and taken control of her toboggan like the French chevaliers she enjoyed reading about in medieval history. The look of intensity and fear etched on Declan's face was one she would never forget.

Her cheeks felt flushed at the memory of the way she'd enthusiastically embraced him in the aftermath of her rescue. She hadn't given a single thought to all of the onlookers. All of a sudden she'd looked up, and Dwight had been standing there. He'd raced all the way down the hill to make sure she was in one piece.

Poor Dwight, she thought. He had looked rather shell-shocked, as if the events of the evening were too much for him to grasp. She felt so guilty. Dwight was her date, but her thoughts were so wrapped up in Declan at the moment, she could barely see straight.

Once the excitement wound down, Dwight walked her back to the concession stand, where word had traveled fast about Declan's quick thinking. Sophie wanted Annie to recount every detail of her escapade. Annie happily complied. She didn't want there to be a single solitary doubt that Declan was a hero. At one point, Sophie sent her a knowing glance that caused her to wonder if she had gushed too much.

Shortly thereafter, Dwight pulled her aside. He had been as quiet as a mouse ever since the toboggan incident.

"Annie, I think I'm going to call it a night," Dwight said in a small voice. He wasn't making eye contact with her, and he appeared to be a million miles away. He didn't seem like his usual confident self. "Will you be able secure a ride home?"

"What? Yes, I can get a ride back to the cabins from Sophie or Hazel. But it's still early, Dwight. Is something wrong? I hope you're not feeling bad about the toboggan. It wasn't your fault."

He looked at her, his brown eyes blinking like an owl. "I saw the way you looked at Declan when he rescued you," Dwight said. "That one look spoke volumes. I'm pretty eager to find love, so I'm not going to waste my time with someone who is so clearly smitten with another man. I'm stepping aside."

Annie didn't bother telling Dwight he was imagining things. Grams had always told her that she wore her heart on her sleeve. Although she wasn't in love with Declan, there were major feelings brewing inside her for him. And the truth was that she was well on her way to being in love with him. Dwight had been nothing but kind to her. At the very least, she owed him the unvarnished truth. "It's nothing against you, Dwight. I met Declan before I even stepped foot into town. It all happened rather quickly. Before I knew it, my feelings for him had grown by leaps and bounds. And there's nothing romantic going on between us. Declan and I are not meant to be together. We're just friends. I promise."

Dwight held up his hand. His features appeared pinched. "Spare me the details. I know women in this town are drawn to men like Declan and Boone and Liam like moths to flames. It seems that young ladies these days go for brawn and chiseled good looks rather than brains and old-fashioned charm," Dwight said in a small voice. "I always try to put my best foot forward, but it doesn't seem to matter when I'm not considered eye candy."

Annie let out a groan. "You're looking at this all wrong. You're you, Dwight. A unique and special individual. That's all you can ever be in this life. Be yourself. And love yourself. That's the perfect road to happiness."

Dwight reached for her mittened hand and brought it up to his lips. "It's been a pleasure, Annie. I wish things could have been different. This town is truly blessed by your presence." With a stately bow, Dwight turned on his heel and departed, leaving her feeling both speechless and saddened. She had accepted Dwight's invitation as a date on a friends-only basis. She hadn't had the heart to say no. Clearly Dwight had been hoping for more to brew between them than friendship, leading to his disappointment when he had come to the realization that she wasn't having the same feelings.

Was it so obvious that she was falling for Declan? Her palms began to sweat as the realization swept over her that Declan himself might have figured it out. That would be all kinds of mortifying.

Annie watched Dwight leave the area and head toward the parking lot. She walked back to the roasting fire, suddenly feeling chilled to the bone. She wrapped her arms around her middle, then rocked back on her heels.

Before she knew it, Declan appeared at her side. His eyes were full of questions.

"Where's your date?" Declan asked, peering behind her as if he was looking for Dwight.

"It appears I've been ditched."

Declan moved toward her, a deep frown etched on his face. "He did what? I've got a good mind to—"

"You'll do no such thing," Annie scolded. "Dwight did what was right. He realized that we were never going to be more than friends. He's quite serious about finding a woman to settle down with, and he wants to move forward in that pursuit."

"When you put it that way, it makes sense," Declan said. "Although he seemed really in to you." He squinted at her. "Are you sure there's not something you're not telling me?" Annie had no intention of telling him what Dwight had sensed about her feelings for Declan. That would be downright embarrassing, especially since she had no idea if Declan had any romantic feelings for her.

Ugh. Why did she suddenly feel as if she had been transported back to high school?

"I've told you the main points. I'm here all alone now with no one to enjoy this beautiful evening with," she hinted. "I'd still like someone to point me toward the northern lights."

He flashed her a magnificent grin. "It would be my pleasure to be your escort," Declan said with a gentlemanly bow. "Declan O'Rourke at your service."

She clapped her hands together and playfully batted her eyelashes. "I thought you'd never ask," she teased.

Declan quirked his mouth. "If you remember, I did ask. You turned me down for Dwight."

She put her hands on her hips. "What kind of woman would I be if I ditched the man I first accepted for the man I wanted to ask me all along?" Annie let out a squeak and slapped her hand over her mouth. Had she really just said that out loud?

Declan's face lit up like Christmas. "So you wanted me to ask you all along, huh?"

Annie groaned. "I hope that doesn't give you a big head. Or should I say, an even bigger head than you already may have?"

He held up his hands. "Hey! I don't have an ego." He snapped the collar on his coat. "I'm not conceited, just convinced."

She swatted at him and laughed. "You have so many women in this town chasing you that it's totally gone to your head."

"There's really only one woman I want to chase me, but something tells me she never would," he said, his blue eyes gleaming with mischief.

Annie felt her cheeks warming up, despite the frigid temperature. Was he referring to her? She ducked her head down to avoid his probing gaze. "Ladies shouldn't pursue," she murmured. "They should be pursued."

"Another Gram-ism?" he asked with a wry smile.

Annie couldn't help but giggle. "I have enough Gram-isms to fill up Kachemak Bay."

Declan didn't laugh. Instead he gazed at her intently, his eyes flashing with an emotion she couldn't quite put her finger on. Suddenly everything hushed and stilled between them. It felt to Annie as if they were the only two people at Deer Run Lake.

He grabbed her hand. "Seeing the northern lights is completely out of our control. There's no way of predicting whether they'll be visible or not. But I know the perfect place to view them if they decide to come out and entertain us."

Adrenaline raced through Annie as Declan led her toward higher ground and a spot on the hill that provided an unobstructed view of the celestial universe. Annie let out a sigh as she gazed up at a velvety sky illuminated by glittery stars and a luminous, fat moon.

"I forgot to tell you my big news." Declan felt as if his chest might burst with pride.

Annie clapped her hands together. Her brown eyes grew wide in her face. "Oh, tell me, Declan. I love happy news."

"I heard from the FAA about the crash. It wasn't my fault. I'm officially cleared," he announced. "It was a bird strike, not pilot error."

Annie let out a hoot and jumped up and down. "That's the best news I've heard in ages. I'm so happy for you."

"Thanks," Declan said, unable to stop himself from grinning ear to ear. "I have to admit, it's a huge relief.

I finally feel as if I can start moving forward and putting all this behind me."

"It's perfect, Declan. Almost as perfect as this Alaskan view. Sky. Moon. Stars. It makes me feel rather insignificant in the scheme of things," Annie said.

He reached out and placed his hands on both sides of her face. "That's the last thing you could ever be, Annie. From the moment I met you, I had a feeling you were going to turn my entire world upside down."

Annie gulped. "Is that a good thing or a bad one?"

"A very wonderful thing." Declan grinned. "This is way overdue. I've been wanting to kiss you since we crash-landed in the Chugach National Forest."

"You have?" she whispered, bowled over by his admission. If Declan had known how many times she'd thought about being kissed by him, he would have been speechless.

"Yes, I have, Annie," he said with a nod, just as he dipped his head down and placed his lips over hers. Declan's lips were warm and inviting and filled with a tenderness that made her soul soar. He tasted like apples and cinnamon. She kissed him back, caught up in this wonderfully romantic moment. A tidal wave of emotion crashed over her as his lips slanted over hers. It had been years since anyone had kissed her. And this wasn't just an ordinary kiss. And Declan O'Rourke wasn't just your average man. He was everything she'd every hoped for wrapped up in the dreamiest of packages.

She would remember this wondrous kiss for the rest of her life. After being duped by love once, Annie had been afraid even to dip her toe into the pond. This kiss…this soul-stirring, amazing kiss…swept her up and carried her to a place she'd only dreamed about. She was soaring way up in the clouds, flying above the earth in a place where nothing could touch her.

As the kiss ended, Annie kept her eyes closed. She didn't want this moment to end. For just a few more seconds, she wanted it to linger so she could savor it all the more. She knew that once she opened her eyes, it would be over and reality would set in. Suddenly she felt Declan's lips tickling her lashes. She let out a giggle. He was kissing her eyelids. When she opened her eyes, he was staring straight at her, a look of wonderment radiating from his eyes.

At that exact moment, Annie knew she was a goner. The kiss had cemented it. There wasn't a single doubt in her mind that she was falling happily, crazily, madly in love with Declan O'Rourke. And it confounded her, because she knew he was the last person in Love who believed in or wanted his own happily-ever-after.

As Declan stood side by side with Annie, gazing up at the vast universe, a feeling of peace settled over him. He'd spent most of his life chasing this feeling. As a kid, he had wanted nothing more than to be surrounded by calm. Yet his world had been filled with chaos. And now, out of the blue, he'd found serenity. It was strange to know with such a deep certainty that God had planted you exactly where you needed to be at exactly the right time.

Raw emotion grabbed him by the throat. It had been such a long while since he'd allowed himself to believe that he deserved happiness. But joy had been all around him tonight, hovering in the air like a promise. Somehow, God was still showing him grace.

Maybe if he stepped out on a leap of faith, he could reach for that elusive dream—home, hearth, a family of his own.

Even though it didn't seem possible, there was a tiny kernel inside him that believed it was possible, after all.

Lord, I need Your grace. I'm so tired of feeling as if the past has already determined my future. I want to be hopeful, not just for everyone around me but for myself as well. I want to be so secure in my faith that I won't question any blessings You bestow on me. And I want the smile on my face to reflect true joy, not just serve as a mask to hide my hurts. I want to be healed, Lord. I want to be hopeful rather than feeling broken.

"Look! A shooting star. I've never seen one before," Annie shouted, pointing up at the onyx sky scattered with stars. "It's on my someday list."

"Your what list?" he asked with a frown. He'd never heard of a someday list.

"My list of things I want to do in my life. It's about two pages, give or take."

Declan smiled. Something told him her list might be a bit longer than two pages. "Well, I guess you can check that one off, huh?"

"Coming here to Love was on my list," she said.

"To find love, huh?" he asked. A tight pressure landed on his chest at the idea of Annie finding love right here in Alaska with an Operation Love participant. He couldn't even pretend that it wouldn't eat him alive.

"Among other things. Starting up the library was very important to me, as is tracing my roots. I've been trying to fill in the blanks ever since I was a kid." Her voice sounded wistful. As light and airy as a fluffy cloud.

"So what did you dream about as a kid?" Declan asked. He could imagine her. Sweet. As smart as a whip. Full of hopes and dreams. Someone who lived by the rules and never colored outside the lines.

Annie looked up at the sky. "All I ever dreamed about was having a family of my own. My mom died when I was two. Gram always said that she died of a broken heart."

"Is that what you believe?" Declan asked. In all his life, he had never heard of a single person dying of heartbreak.

She nodded. "Yes. I do. My dad captured my mother's heart, but he didn't stick around very long. Even though she was pregnant with his child, he never bothered to marry my mom. Even though he abandoned us, she still loved him until the day she died. He charmed his way right into her heart. So…because my Gram was a single mother, then my mom, I always wanted to be married with a family." Her voice cracked. She bowed her head. "That probably sounds silly to you."

His throat clogged up. "No, it doesn't sound silly at all." A sharp sensation pierced his chest, and he found himself wishing that he could give her all her hopes and dreams wrapped up in a big bright bow. If only it were that simple. If only he could.

"I found a lot of my dreams at the library. Books carried me away to other worlds. When I was reading *Jane Eyre*, I became her. And I lived vicariously through her adventures. Reading about foreign lands made me dream of traveling all over the world. It made me want to live courageously. Knowing that books can transform lives made me want to become a librarian." She turned toward him, her face lit up by the soft glow of the moon.

"What about you? Were your dreams always filled with flying?" Annie asked. "Or did you aspire to take the medical world by storm or become a firefighter?"

"From the time I knew what airplanes did, I wanted to be a pilot. When I was a kid, I used to dream about touching the sky. Once I flew my first plane, I was hooked. Soaring up in the air made me feel connected to something much larger than myself." He flashed back to some of his first flying outings with his father. In his eyes, Colin O'Rourke had been the coolest, fiercest pilot in the whole wide world. He never would have able to imagine his father's dramatic fall from grace or how the man he adored would change so drastically.

"I've never been able to put into words why I love being up there so much. All I know is that when I'm up there, thousands of feet off the ground, I feel freer than I've ever felt with my legs firmly planted on the ground. And each and every time, I've known God was with me." He shrugged. "I can't explain it very well in words. It's just a feeling, I guess."

"It sounds a lot like faith to me. He's always with us," Annie reminded him. "Even when we think He might not be."

"I've had a lot of moments in my life when I've doubted God's presence. Sometimes things happen that are so mind-numbingly awful, it makes you think you're crazy to believe at all."

Annie nodded. "I know. After Gram's accident, I kept asking God why He left me all alone. I had to remind myself that He had blessed me with her in the first place. Grief is the price we pay for loving and being loved. And given the choice, I'd choose love every single time."

Her words served as a sucker punch. All of his feelings were riding right on the surface tonight. And now, his thoughts were gravitating toward the huge losses in his own life. The death of his mother had left a terrible wound. Even now, some twenty years later, there was still a festering sore surrounding her death.

He locked gazes with Annie. "I was eight when my mother died. It was hard to wrap my head around losing her so suddenly. One minute she was tucking us into bed, and the next we were being woken up in the middle of the night to a nightmare come to life. All I really remember is this overwhelming feeling of grief and sadness that hung over us like a dark cloud." He took a deep breath to fortify himself. This wasn't a topic he ever discussed, not even with Finn, who had been just as deeply affected by the loss of their mother.

"We didn't talk about it in our house. I heard whispers here in town. Hushed voices. But back at home, it was almost as if she had fallen into this big black hole and was whisked away from us."

Annie reached out and squeezed his hand. "Eight is such a tender age, Declan. Way too young to grapple with such a devastating loss."

He swung his gaze toward Annie. Her eyes were full of so much compassion. He prayed she wouldn't be horrified by what he was about to say next. It was pressing on his heart to unburden himself.

"Her death should never have happened. It was senseless and stupid and it tore me apart. My parents had both been drinking that night. Finn and I were asleep in our beds. They were goofing around in the backyard with a rifle, trying to shoot tin cans. My dad made some stupid comment about shooting a raccoon that ran across the yard, and she pulled the gun away from him. It went off and shot her in the stomach. She died right there in the yard."

Declan would never forget being woken up by Finn or the desperate cries of his father as the tragedy was unfolding. He'd never told a single soul about how he had wandered into the backyard and witnessed his father cradling his dying mother in his arms. No, that particular memory had been locked away inside the vault, never to see the light of day. He had never even shared it with Boone. As it was, it had already been seared into his memory for all eternity. His lovely, kind mother taking her last breaths with his father's name on her lips.

"Oh, Declan. I'm so sorry. That's horrific. And to lose her so suddenly like that is unimaginable," she said. Annie sniffed back tears.

"I wish I could remember more about her. Her name was Cindy. She was funny. And she used to make us peanut-butter cookies after school. And she used to fly down Cupid's Hill like lightning without an ounce of fear. She was my mom, and I loved her very much." He let out a ragged sigh. "I hate being part of something so ugly."

"I hope you know that what happened that night doesn't define you. It sounds like it was a terrible, tragic accident."

He stared off into the distance. "One that ripped

our childhood apart. From that day on, I never felt completely safe again."

"That's understandable," she said in a soft voice. "Life as you knew it came to a crashing halt."

"My father—" Declan began. He looked shaken. Annie reached out and squeezed his hand through his gloves.

"We don't have to talk about this," she said in a soft voice.

"It's okay," he said, a sheen of moisture in his eyes. "After my mom died, he wasn't a father to us. He went inward to a place where we couldn't reach him. My parents were childhood sweethearts. Her dying like that buried him under a mountain…of loss, I guess you could say."

"And guilt, too, I imagine," she murmured. "It wasn't his fault, but he may have assumed ownership of it."

"He started drinking a lot and road-tripping, sometimes for weeks at a time. He began hanging out with a rough crowd in Anchorage. He got mixed up in a store burglary that went horribly wrong. One of his cohorts shot a store keeper. My dad was sentenced to ten years for being an accomplice. His sentence was cut down to eight for good behavior."

He heard Annie suck in a deep breath. Her lips trembled while tears ran down her cheeks. Declan worried that he had overwhelmed her with his tragic story. It was a lot to hear in one sitting. "I can't imagine how difficult it must have been to go through this. My heart aches for that eight-year-old little boy whose world was rocked by such tragedy."

"Thank you, Annie. For listening. And for being so understanding."

For years he had tried to stuff all the bad experiences down and hide behind a joke and a smile. The truth was that he had been deeply altered by his family's tragedy. The ripples had kept coming until he'd almost been pulled under by the tide.

"What about your father? Where is he now?" Annie asked. Her voice sounded hesitant, as if she hadn't been entirely certain if she should pose this question.

He let out a harsh laugh. "One would imagine that after all that time separated from his kids, he would have come back home to Love." Declan let out a harsh laugh. "Nope. He kept right on going, never quite making it back here to reunite with us. We were blessed that Grandpop stepped in and raised us. He taught me everything I needed to know about flying. And plenty more about life. I can never thank him enough. When he passed away, the Prescotts took me in."

"What about Finn?" she asked. Surely he'd been able to cling to his brother in such a time of turmoil.

"He took off as soon as he turned eighteen. Nothing and no one could keep him here in Love. He's a lot like my dad in that respect. Always on the move. Never staying in any one place long enough to put down roots." Even when Declan had begged him to stay, Finn had shrugged him off and done as he pleased. He'd needed Finn after his grandfather's passing, but all his brother had wanted to do was escape.

"Running away from it all," Annie murmured. "Sounds like that's his coping mechanism."

"Yep," Declan said with a sigh. "And my dad is out

there somewhere in the world, trying to find his own semblance of peace, I imagine."

"Let's pray he finds it," Annie said as she reached for his hand. "Living your life with one foot in the past isn't really living at all."

It was as if Annie was speaking directly to him with her heartfelt words. Did she see past his veneer? Did she sense that his whole life had been built on a shaky foundation due to his traumatic past?

He wished with all his might that he could be different. Not just for her, but for himself as well. For so long, he had prayed to God about moving forward without carrying the weight of his father's actions on his shoulders. He wished that he could be the man Annie deserved, one who didn't question whether he could go the distance with her or provide her with the life she had been dreaming about since she was a little girl. When he closed his eyes and tried to imagine their life unfolding together, all he came up with was a blank.

Despite the overwhelming feelings that Annie was stirring up inside him, Declan still couldn't imagine himself walking off into the sunset with the woman of his dreams. And that simple fact left him feeling shaky and uncertain. It had been such a wonderful evening, yet harsh reality had suddenly settled in and crashed over him in unrelenting waves. He felt as if someone had thrown a bucket of cold water over him. Sneaking in a kiss with Annie had been wonderful, but it wasn't something that he could ever allow to happen again after this evening.

The night was no longer young. Against the backdrop of a velvety sky, the townsfolk began to pack up their belongings and call it a night. Declan pitched in with the cleanup as he replayed the events of the evening in his mind's eye.

Annie had gone home with Sophie. At first he'd wanted to insist on dropping Annie off at the Black Bear Cabins, but one look at Sophie and Annie convinced him that the two women deserved some bonding time. Annie needed girlfriends in Love, ones she could confide in and laugh with and get advice from about long Alaskan winters and being homesick for the lower forty-eights.

He wanted to kiss her again, but he knew it wouldn't be fair to lead her down that path when she'd made it clear she had come to Alaska for the whole nine yards—love, a husband and a white picket fence. None of those things were in his repertoire. And he'd rather cut off his right arm than break Annie's heart. It was way better to quit while he was ahead.

"I've been looking for you." Boone walked up and clapped Declan on the back as he loaded up one of the vans used to transport items to the party. He pulled him over to an isolated area, where it was just the two of them. "Hey! What's this I hear about you lowering your insurance premium on Lucy?"

Declan groaned. "I see you've been talking to Finn. He sure didn't waste any time in spreading it around." It annoyed him to no end that Finn had divulged his insurance information to Boone without even checking in with him first. Who did Finn think he was? Declan seethed.

Boone frowned. "Telling your best friend isn't exactly gossiping. He's worried about you. And so am I. I've got some money in my savings account. It probably won't be enough to cover the total cost, but it'll help."

Declan shook his head. "You can't keep throwing me lifelines. You have Grace now and a baby on the way," Declan protested. "I appreciate the offer, but I can't go down that road."

"Well, then, what are you doing to do?" Boone asked.

Declan shrugged. "There's no need to worry. Yet."

Boone raised an eyebrow. "What does that even mean?"

He ran his hand over his face. "It means that everything in my life is in turmoil at the moment, but I'm trying not to panic. Even though I just found out that the accident was due to a bird strike, that doesn't solve all my problems. I need a substantial amount of money to make up the difference between the insurance payout and the cost of a new seaplane. I've been canceling flights and having jitters about getting back up in the air."

Compassion flickered in Boone's eyes. "It's only natural to feel a bit skittish after being in a plane crash," Boone conceded, "but you've got to get back in the cockpit, Declan. Don't let fear take away the thing you most enjoy."

Declan threw his hands in the air. "And to make things even more complicated, I kissed Annie tonight."

Boone narrowed his gaze. "And that's a bad thing? I like Annie. She's genuine. And smart." He winked at Declan. "And very easy on the eyes."

"She's all those things and more. But she's not ever going to be anything more than a friend. She came to this town to find a groom, not a broken-down pilot who can't commit to a woman to save his life."

Boone loudly sucked his teeth. "That's garbage, and you know it! You're just as worthy of a wife and family as I am. There's no one who is more loyal or devoted than you. I don't understand why you can't move forward."

Declan swung his gaze up to meet Boone's probing gaze. "You know why."

Boone let out a huge sigh. "You can't let your past determine your future. The sins of the father should not be visited on the child. Remember that Bible verse?"

He scoffed. "Remember it? It's been in my head since I was eight years old."

A tremor ran along Boone's jaw. "Don't you think it's time you got past it?" His voice came out ragged. "Imagine what might happen if you just free yourself from all these chains that are tying you down. You might soar."

He shook his head fiercely. Every time he visualized doing so, he found himself wondering what would happen if it all fell apart. If he messed things up. "Not at her expense. I don't want to hurt her."

"You won't. I've seen the way you look at her. It's stamped all over your face that you think she hung the moon," Boone insisted.

He let out a huff of air. "I don't deserve her! Is that what you want me to say, Boone? Is that what you want to hear?"

Boone grabbed him by the shoulders and shook him. "No! Because it's not true. It's just this great big lie that you tell yourself," he growled. "I want you to man up and face this thing down before it knocks you off course with Annie. Because something tells me that if you let this moment pass you by, you'll always regret it."

A sharp pain twisted Declan's insides. "Maybe," he acknowledged. "But I'll never forgive myself if I make her think I'm something I'm not. She wants it all. The white picket fence. The adoring husband. Two-point-five kids. The whole nine yards. Face it, Boone. My happily-ever-after died a long time ago."

Without a word of goodbye, Declan walked off into the Alaskan night with his hands jammed into his pockets, his head bowed to protect himself against the sharp wind that had suddenly kicked up. He heard Boone call after him, but he didn't bother to turn around. There was nothing his best friend could say to change a single thing.

Without even meaning to, he had reached out for something with Annie that he knew was beyond his grasp. From this point forward, he wasn't going to make that mistake. Not ever again. It hurt way too much to come crashing down to reality.

Chapter Eleven

"So, what's the verdict?" Cameron stood next to Declan's table at the Moose Café the morning after the skating party, his arms folded across his chest. His friend's face was filled with expectation.

"Give me a second. I haven't even tasted it yet." Declan bit into the chive, Swiss cheese and ham omelet. He let out a groan. It was out of this world. Cameron had outdone himself with breakfast this morning.

Cameron nodded his head and grinned. "I told you. This is going on the menu, effective immediately." He slapped Declan on the back. "Thanks for being my tester. You always come through."

"Anytime," Declan called out as Cameron walked back toward the kitchen with an extra bit of pep in his step. Declan loved being a tester at the Moose Café. More times than not, he loved the food Cameron dished up. Plus it was all on the house. In Declan's world, it didn't get any better than that.

His phone began vibrating in his jacket pocket. He'd placed the phone on Vibrate so he could enjoy his breakfast in peace without interruption. With a sigh of frustration, he reached into his pocket and yanked out the phone, answering in a curt voice.

"O'Rourke here."

"Declan, it's Willard. I've been calling you all morning. I can't make the run today." A loud sneeze rang out. "Liam just diagnosed me with flu."

Declan's pulse raced. His palms became sweaty, and he could hear his heart thundering in his ears. "Are you sure?"

"Yes, I'm sure. I have a fever of a hundred and three with vomiting and nausea. I think that rules me out, Declan."

"Sorry, buddy. Feel better, okay?" Declan said before ending the call. The moment he disconnected, he sat back in his chair and heaved a tremendous sigh. Suddenly he had lost his appetite.

Willard was too sick to fly today. What was Declan going to do now? He shoved a hand through his rumpled head of hair. O'Rourke Charters really needed the income. He couldn't afford to blow this off. He held his hands out in front of him. Just the thought of flying Ethel was causing them to tremble like crazy.

"Fancy meeting you here."

Declan jerked his head up at the sweet-sounding voice that had invaded his dreams last night. Annie was standing beside his table, looking gorgeous in a white wool dress and the pair of boots he'd gifted her. She had a long black coat draped over her arm.

"What's up with your hands?" She jutted her chin at him.

"Oh, it's nothing," he said, trying to sound casual.

She tapped her booted foot on the hardwood floor. "Tell that to someone else, O'Rourke. What's wrong?"

He met her steely gaze. "I'm just a little stressed out at the moment. My employee, Willard, just called me. He's too sick with flu to fly our client to Homer today, which is a big deal." He glanced at his watch. "The flight leaves in an hour. Canceling this gig would hurt our bottom line, since this is a regular customer who spends a lot of money on travel."

"Well then, Declan, you're just going to have to fly the client yourself," Annie said in a no-nonsense voice.

He shook his head. "I can't do it. I'm not ready yet," he said, his tone clipped.

Annie reached out and began tugging him by the wrist. Yikes. She was way stronger than she looked.

"Hey! What are you doing?" Declan cried out as he resisted her efforts to displace him from his seat. "I'm in the middle of breakfast."

Annie let go of him. She placed her hands on her hips. Her brown eyes flashed. "I'm getting you mobilized. Step away from the omelet, O'Rourke. You have a client who is paying you good money to fly to Homer in approximately one hour."

"Me? You think I'm going to fly Ethel? I'm not ready to take this on," he admitted as a feeling of shame threatened to swallow him whole.

"Willard is sick with the flu, which means it's all on your shoulders. There's no one else but you."

"I'm not sure I can do it, Annie." What was the point of pretending anymore? It was high time he came clean. He was fairly certain Annie already knew that his fear was preventing him from flying Ethel.

"What aren't you sure about? Your skill? Your expertise? Your perfect flying record? The fact that you now know that you had nothing to do with the malfunctioning of your plane? It was a random bird strike. Something rare and completely out of your control."

"So what if it happens again?" he spit out.

She shrugged. "So what if the sky falls? You can drum up hundreds of scenarios to convince yourself not to do something. Don't give in to the fear. It will consume you if you let it."

"Live courageously," Declan said. He'd been hearing Annie say this for weeks now. In this very moment, it resonated with him. That's how he wanted to live his life. Without fear or reservations. Flying was his world. He could never be whole if he hid in the shadows and stayed grounded.

"Exactly!" Annie said. "You've got this!"

"No one handed me O'Rourke Charters," he said in a raised voice.

"Nope," Annie said. "You didn't grow up with a silver spoon in your mouth."

"I built my company through hard work and grit and determination," he said.

"Yes, you did!" Annie encouraged him. "And you're not going to throw it in the toilet simply because you have a few jitters. Declan O'Rourke is not going out like that!"

"No, he's not," Hazel chimed in as she appeared at the table with a basket of corn bread in her hands. "If he does, he'll have me to deal with."

"You better listen to Hazel." Annie scrunched up her nose and made a face. "Those are fighting words!"

"Did anyone ever tell you that you're one beautiful pain in the neck?" Declan asked in a raspy tone as he stood up from his chair.

"Maybe once or twice," Annie murmured as he dipped his head and kissed her soundly on the lips.

"Enough smooching, you two, 'cause time is a wasting," Hazel barked. "It waits for no man...or woman. One of these days Jasper will figure that out before the best years of my life have passed me by," she grumbled.

"He still isn't ready to put a ring on it?" Declan asked, his eyebrows raised.

"Ha! A ring?" Hazel shouted. "At this point I'd settle for a quickie wedding in Vegas and a piece of tinfoil on my finger."

Annie made a tutting sound. "Don't settle for anything, Hazel. You deserve a swoon-worthy proposal and a wedding with all the trimmings. And some bling on your ring finger."

Hazel reached out and squeezed Annie's hand. "You're some kind of special, Annie." Her voice was choked with emotion. Her eyes radiated warmth.

"Annie's right, Hazel," Declan said, reaching across and pressing a kiss on her cheek. "If Jasper can't see what a gem you are, then he's a plumb fool."

"You're a sweetheart, Declan," Hazel said with tears in her eyes. "I'm so proud of you. For facing your fears and tackling them head-on. That's never easy, even for an old bird like me."

Declan reached out and hugged the woman who was the closest thing to a mother figure he had in his life. She'd always been there for him, firmly rooted in his corner. Just like Boone and his family. "Aw, Hazel. Please don't cry," he said, wrapping her up in a tight bear hug. "You're going to make me cry, too," he teased.

"Why don't you finish that omelet before Cameron has a conniption fit," Hazel said with a laugh. "If it's okay, I'd like to pray over your food. Why don't we sit down for a minute."

They sat down at the table. Hazel reached for their hands, and they made a circle at the table as she prayed over Declan's meal. "Dear Lord, please bless this food. And please bless and protect Declan as he makes this flight to Homer. May his skill and precision as a pilot shine today brighter than ever. Amen."

Once breakfast was finished, Annie rode over to the pier with Declan in his truck. Afterward, she would make the short walk from the pier over to the library to open it up and begin her shift.

"You've got this!" Annie encouraged him as he walked toward Ethel, followed closely by his clients, a mother-daughter duo who had been sightseeing in Love.

Declan turned around and flashed her a thumbs-up sign. "You know it," he said. "I'm right where I need to be, thanks to you."

Once he settled himself into the cockpit, Declan felt a surge of adrenaline pounding through his veins. He fingered the controls and smiled at the excitement rising up within him. It was always like this when he was about to take one of his planes up in the wild blue yonder.

As he soared into the sky, Declan cast his gaze out the window. Usually he focused on what was above and around him. Endless sky. Cotton ball–like fluffy clouds. What lay past the horizon. This time he found himself looking down and searching for a glimpse of Annie. He spotted her, a small speck of red in a sea of white. A feeling of joy fluttered through him. He was soaring. Gliding. And it felt invigorating to be sitting in the cockpit, at the controls, flying his beloved Ethel. None of this would have happened today if it hadn't been for Annie. *Plucky, adorable Annie.* She had forced him out of his comfort zone this morning, all because she cared about him and O'Rourke Charters. Annie wanted the best for him. And she had just proved to him that she would go the extra mile to make sure that all was right in his world.

As he soared higher and higher up in the sky, past the clouds and the mountains and on toward Homer, he rejoiced in the sensation of being on top of the world. At the same time he suspected he was falling...tumbling... headlong over the edge for Annie.

Annie looked around her at the library patrons who were browsing the shelves. It made her smile to see people enjoying the library with such enthusiasm. These days it seemed as if she wore a perpetual smile on her face. Ever since Declan had reestablished his flying routine a week ago, things between them had been better than ever. Declan seemed to radiate a confidence that took her breath away. More and more it seemed as if he believed in himself. And she was beginning to believe in them, even though it went against her nature to hope for things that were out of her grasp. The very words she'd tossed at Declan were beginning to resonate deeply within her.

Living your life with one foot in the past isn't really living at all.

She had been guilty this whole time of the same exact thing. Her past relationship with Todd had jaded her about good-looking men like Declan. Being duped by him had left an emotional scar on her heart. Her desire not to repeat the cycle in her family of unwed mothers had made her overly cautious. It shamed her to realize that she had judged Declan based on his looks and his flirtatious ways.

She had always been a fair-minded person. Had she been just in her view of Declan?

Declan was handsome and charming. That in itself wasn't a crime. They were simply two of the many reasons she loved him. *Loved him?*

Annie stopped in her tracks and placed the books she was holding onto the shelf. Her legs were trembling underneath her.

Love! Did she really love Declan? Yes! She loved him with every fiber of her being. Wholly. Devotedly. Without reservation.

He was coming over tonight for dinner. She was putting her best culinary foot forward and making him Gram's famous chicken parmesan. And she was going to talk to him about Gram's journal and her plans to approach Mayor Prescott about his relationship with her grandmother. It was time! The longer she waited, the more explaining she would have to do about why she hadn't introduced herself as Aurelia Alice Murray's granddaughter when she'd arrived in Love.

A feeling of excitement thrummed in her veins. Everything was falling perfectly into line. O'Rourke Charters was back on track, and her quest to find her family would soon come to an end. By the time Declan arrived at her cabin, she had put the finishing touches on dinner and set the table to create an intimate, romantic vibe. She bit her lip as she surveyed the vase of flowers and the woodsy scented candles. She didn't want Declan to think she was trying too hard. A sudden knock on the door made it a moot point. Declan had arrived, bearing a box of pastries from the Moose Café.

"Wow. This place looks terrific. You've really transformed it," Declan said as he looked around. She followed his gaze as he surveyed the cabin. She had put a lot of love and care into creating a chic vibe in the once-drab cabin. New curtains, rugs, throw covers, lamps. The whole nine yards.

"Thanks. Hazel almost didn't recognize it when she came inside the other day. And Sophie wants me to refurbish her room when I get some spare time," Annie said with a chuckle.

Declan winked at her. "Sounds like you might have a good side business going there."

"I have something to tell you," she said. She could barely contain her excitement. "It's about Gram's journal."

"Oh. Before I forget, I brought it back." He reached down to the inside pocket of his jacket and pulled it out.

"Thank you," she said, placing the diary down onto the table. "I've decided to approach Jasper about being his granddaughter."

Declan's eyes went wide. He frowned at her. "What are you going to say, Annie?"

"That we're related," she said with a wide spreading motion of her arms. "The town council has requested my presence at their meeting tomorrow to discuss the literacy program, so I was thinking I might pull him aside afterward and tell him."

"Annie, I don't think you should say anything." Declan's tone sounded somber.

Perhaps she had misheard him? What was Declan hinting at?

Annie cocked her head to the side. "What? Why, of course I should. That's been my plan this entire time. Jasper has a right to know who I am and that I might be his granddaughter."

"I understand why you think this is a good idea, but let me tell you why it's not." He inhaled deeply. "If what you're saying is true, Jasper would have been married to Harmony at the time your mother was conceived. They were married right after high school. The implication would be that he betrayed his wife and his wedding vows."

Annie bristled. She hadn't considered that fact, and her mind was now whirling with the implications. Now she had some insight into why Gram might have left Love. Being pregnant by a married man would have rocked the small fishing village.

"It's far from ideal, but it doesn't change the fact that the Prescott family might be kin to me."

"Might," Declan bit out. "Do you really want to open a can of worms for a *might*?"

Can of worms? Was that what he thought about her search for her roots?

He reached for her hand. "I know you don't want to hurt the Prescotts."

She pulled her hand away from him. "I'm not trying to hurt anyone. I just want to know who I am and where I come from," she sobbed. "That has nothing to do with anyone but me."

"It's not that simple. I've known this family my

whole life. This would tear them apart. You probably don't know this, but the female exodus from Love began decades ago, around the time Harmony left town. She died after she left Alaska. Her death occurred before they could patch things up and Jasper could bring her home. My point is…the Prescotts have already been through the ringer. Boone and his siblings had to endure their parents' divorce, Liam and Aidan losing Ruby, Jasper's heart attack, the recession here in town, Boone and Honor being estranged from one another. And Cameron just got his life back after being blamed for the cannery deal that went bust."

Everything stilled and hushed for Annie. She had heard every word Declan had uttered about the Prescott family. He was making it crystal clear for her. The feelings of his surrogate family mattered way more than her quest to find her family roots. For Declan, it wasn't even a close contest. He was striving to keep his beloved family from being hurt, at her expense. A sharp pain sliced her midsection. She wrapped her arms around her middle, wishing she could make these painful feelings disappear.

"I've been through a lot, too. I lost my mother, Grams…and I never had a father," she said in a dazed voice. How could Declan so easily discount her sorrows?

"I know you have, Annie. And I can't tell you how sorry I am about those losses. I'm not telling you what to do—" Declan began.

"Aren't you?" she snapped. "How long have I been asking you for your opinion about Gram's diary? And you've been stalling me, no doubt because you didn't want to have to tell me that you also believe Jasper is my grandfather. Isn't that right?"

Declan looked away from her. She let out a harsh laugh and shook her head. All day she had been anticipating this evening, imagining it would turn out to be a very special night for the two of them. And now everything had crumbled into dust.

"I think you should leave, Declan," she said in a cold voice that brooked no argument.

Declan's eyes flickered with hurt. "Annie! Let's talk about this."

"I've heard more than enough! Don't worry about it. You've made yourself quite clear." Annie marched toward the door and wrenched it open. Declan waited a few beats, then made his way to her side. He reached out and grazed her cheek with his finger. "None of this was meant to hurt you, Annie." Declan moved toward the threshold and walked into the bitter chill of the Alaskan night. Before she could make a fool of herself and openly sob in front of him, Annie slammed the door behind Declan and crumpled to the floor. Huge sobs racked her body as she chided herself for ever having fallen for Declan O'Rourke.

Chapter Twelve

The following day, all Declan could do to avoid wallowing in his misery was to focus on O'Rourke Charters and his clients. Problem was, every time he did so, thoughts of Annie hovered over him like a shroud. He pressed his eyes closed as the painful memories from last night washed over him with the force of a tsunami. It didn't take a rocket scientist to figure out that he had messed up royally. His love and protectiveness for the Prescott family had clashed with his love for Annie.

Declan was in love with Annie. For the first time in his life, he could say those words with conviction. He loved Annie. Loved. Adored.

But the events of last night now stood between them. He had been about as subtle as a sledgehammer in his approach. Every single word he had uttered had come out wrong. And the more he opened his mouth, the worse it got. By the time she had asked him to leave, he had been in a state of shock. What in the world had he done?

He had a life full of all the things a man could ever

need. His own business. A home. Loyal friends. All except one thing. He didn't have Annie. He didn't have the woman he loved by his side. And it hurt. The pain seared his insides.

Annie had been absolutely right about being stuck in the past. For so long now, he'd had one foot stuck in the past while trying to move toward his future. Now, because of Annie, he wanted to say goodbye to all those dark memories and embrace the future. Their future. The white picket fence. A home in the woods. Whatever it took to make Annie happy and fulfilled.

A quick look at his watch confirmed that the town-council meeting was still in session. He needed to be there. But first, he needed to dig into his sock drawer and pull out his mother's most precious possession. Hopefully by the end of the evening it would be twinkling from Annie's ring finger.

The sound of a motorcycle cut into the silence. He let out a groan as he stuffed the ring box into his jacket pocket. Finn always did have bad timing.

His front door burst open without any warning.

"Hey!" Declan cried out as his brother crashed into his house. "Knock before you storm in here. Okay?"

Finn walked right up to him and poked him in the chest. "You need to listen to a few things I have to say."

He pushed his finger away. "Finn, I'm on my way out. I have a very serious matter to attend to at the town-council meeting."

"I'm not going to let you blow me off." Finn raked his hand through his tousled mane of brown hair. "I know you need a new plane. I'm offering you an opportunity to let me buy my way into O'Rourke Charters."

Declan simply stared at Finn. He was dumbfounded. Had he heard him right? Finn wanted another opportunity to be a part of O'Rourke Charters?

Finn held up his hands. "I know what you're going to say. That I never stick around. That I bailed on you the last time. Well, you're wrong. I actually just bought a little place. A fixer-upper. I'm here to stay, Declan. And I want to partner up with you."

A few months ago Declan might have viewed Finn's proposal as crazy. So much had changed in the last few weeks. He'd lost Lucy. He had been in his first plane crash. And he'd fallen hopelessly in love with Annie Murray. All those things had transformed him. He didn't want to hold Finn's past actions against him. Finn was family.

"Come up with a proposal for me to look at, Finn. And if you're serious about buying into the company, you're going to have to secure financing."

Finn's mouth hung open. "You're okay with this?"

Declan nodded. "We'll have to work out the details. As long as your proposal looks good, I'm open to all the possibilities."

Finn let out a whoop of excitement and lifted Declan off the ground. "Put me down, Finn. Seriously. I have to be somewhere. It's urgent."

Finn regarded him curiously. "Is there a fire you need to put out or something? You look like you're about to jump out of your skin."

"No," Declan grunted. "I need to go find the woman I love and tell her that I'm the world's biggest fool."

Annie was doing her very best to focus on the town meeting. Much to her dismay, every other second she found herself distracted by thoughts of Declan. At some point she needed to figure out how she was going to get over him. There was no way in the world she intended to pine for a man who stood in the way of her dreams.

Impossible. How could she convince her heart not to love him? She'd had no control over it in the first place, after all. Her love for him had blossomed without any assistance from her. She let out a sigh. Perhaps it would be best to start dating some men in town. It would serve as a nice diversion. And who knew? Maybe she would fall in love with someone else.

Tears gathered in her eyes as her heart handily rejected that notion. It was Declan who held her heart in the palm of his hand. And she feared it would always be Declan who made her soul soar.

The sound of footsteps beside her aisle seat caused her to swing her gaze upward. Declan was standing beside her, staring at her with mournful eyes.

He looked over at the dais where the town-council members were seated. "Jasper," he called out. "Our town librarian has something she needs to ask you."

"No, I don't," Annie said in a loud whisper, shooting Declan her fiercest glare.

What was Declan doing by showing up here and interrupting the meeting?

"Now's your opportunity to say what's resting on your heart," he told her in a low voice.

Of all the nerve! He was now pushing her out on the ledge after he'd told her last night not to pursue the matter.

Jasper beckoned her to the dais. "Come on. Don't be shy, Annie. We're old friends now, right?"

Dwight slammed his palm down on the dais. "This is yet another example of a complete and utter lack of civility and violating the rules of order. I heartily object to these shenanigans."

"Sorry, Dwight," Declan said in a raised voice, "but sometimes there are things that are way more important than being a rule keeper."

"Such as?" Dwight asked. "Please enlighten me." His voice oozed sarcasm.

"Such as righting a wrong," Declan said in a tender voice. His eyes flickered with an emotion that caused Annie's heart to thump wildly. He reached out, grasped her hand in his and tugged until she was standing up. "I was wrong. Stupendously, dreadfully wrong. Asking you not to pursue your family connections here in Love was selfish. I was afraid that you might hurt people I love. But in silencing you, I did the very thing I was trying to avoid. I hurt you. I never want to see that look in your eyes again."

"Family connections?" Jasper asked in a thunderous voice. "What in the world are you talking about?"

"Annie," Declan said gently. "I think it's time you spoke your piece. You've waited so long for this moment.

She turned toward Declan, suddenly consumed by doubts. What if she was wrong? What if she made a colossal fool of herself? She had never imagined this scene unfolding in such a public place, with so many eyes trained on her. "I don't know what to say," she whispered. Declan squeezed her hand tightly.

"Speak from your heart." He winked at her. "You've always been good at that."

Emboldened by Declan's support, Annie swung her

gaze toward Jasper. "My grandmother was born and raised in this town. Thanks to her stories, I loved this village well before I ever stepped off Declan's seaplane. Her name was Aurelia Alice Murray."

Shocked gasps rang out in the room. Jasper's blue eyes bulged. He sputtered. "You're Alice's kin? Her granddaughter?"

Annie felt as if someone had taken a great weight off her chest. Keeping this secret hadn't been easy. "Yes," she said with a nod. "I am."

"Why in the world didn't you say something when you got here? Alice was a hometown gal. She was a dear friend of mine and of plenty of other folks in this town."

Annie turned toward Declan. His eyes radiated encouragement. "You can do this. Live courageously. Remember why you came to Love in the first place."

Live courageously. It had been her motto from the very beginning. She needed to live it.

"Spit it out, Annie. Some of us aren't getting any younger, in case you hadn't noticed," Jasper barked.

"Speak up!" someone shouted from the crowd.

Declan stepped forward and stood in front of Annie. "Give her a break. Let her say what she has to say without being badgered or screamed at."

Boone sent Declan an approving nod. Declan pulled Annie forward by the wrist and stood beside her, bolstering her by his presence.

"Gram died last year. One of the reasons I came here was because I grew up hearing all about her beloved hometown." She struggled to speak past the lump in her throat. "I wanted to fill that void inside me by connecting with the place that shaped her early years. I also wanted to find my grandfather."

"Grandfather!" Jasper bellowed. "Who is your grandfather?"

Feeling brave, Annie took a few steps forward so that she was standing directly in front of Jasper and looking up at him on the dais. Their gazes locked. Confusion swirled in his blue eyes. "I think you are, Mayor Prescott."

Chaos erupted in the town hall meeting room as soon as Annie dropped her bombshell. Jasper's mouth gaped. Hazel shot him an incredulous look. Boone frowned. Dwight began coughing uncontrollably.

Boone folded his arms across his chest. "So, Jasper, care to explain?"

Jasper rolled his eyes at his grandson. "I'm sorry, young lady, but I'm not your grandfather. I know this for a fact. You see, I met my wife, Harmony, when I was a small boy. I can firmly attest to the fact that love at first sight does exist. It happened to me when I first saw Harmony. And from the time I was fortunate enough to win her love till the day she died, I never looked at another woman. Not a look. Not a held hand. Not a kiss. Nothing." He spread his hands wide. "So you see, it's impossible that you belong to me."

Tears coursed down Annie's face. Her shoulders shook with sobs. This had been the very thing she had been so afraid of. Crushed dreams. Disappointment.

"I just wanted to find my roots so I could be connected with someone here in Love," Annie sobbed.

Jasper walked down from the dais and wrapped Annie up in his arms. He patted her back and said in a soothing voice, "Any man would be happy to claim you for a granddaughter. You're a wonderful young woman, Annie. This town is proud to call you a resident."

"Th-thank you, Mayor Prescott," she said through sniffles. "You're very kind.

He tipped her chin up to meet his regard. "What's with this Mayor Prescott business? We're old friends now. Call me Jasper."

"I wish you were my grandfather." She whispered the words so softly that she wasn't certain he even heard her.

"I may not be your grandfather, but I think I can steer you in the direction of who is," he said with a broad smile. "And he's a good, God-fearing man."

"Wh-what?" Annie cried. "Really? You know who he is?"

"He's right behind you, Annie. And unless I'm mistaken, I think he's coming to claim you."

Declan whirled around at the same time as Annie. There wasn't a single sound in the room. Everyone was watching as Zachariah slowly made his way to the front of the room with the use of his cane. He came to a stop right in front of her. A stunned expression was etched on his face. "At my age, surprises are few and far between. I can't quite believe this is happening," he said in an awed voice.

"Me, neither," she said, noticing for the first time that Zachariah had kind eyes. "Were you and Gram in love?"

"Yes, we were, Annie. Very much in love," he said.

He let out a ragged sigh. "But like life often is…it was complicated."

"Complicated by what?" Annie asked.

"Petty jealousies and judgments and immaturity. Not to mention false pride." A petite woman with silver-gray hair stepped forward from the audience. Annie let out a gasp as the woman came into view. Her resemblance to Gram was startling. They shared the same blue eyes, the same striking hair color and similar features.

The woman grasped her by the hand. "I knew your grandmother almost as well as I knew myself. My name is Cilla. And Alice was my sister."

Sister? Gram had never mentioned a sister! Annie felt as if she'd fallen down the rabbit hole and entered a whole new world.

Zachariah shook his head. "Your grandmother was my sweetie. I made the fool mistake of breaking up with Alice. I was young and foolish, and I resisted the idea of settling down," Zachariah said. "When you're young and immature, sometimes you think sowing your wild oats is of vital importance." He let out a ragged sigh. "For a time there, Alice kept running after me, trying to convince me to take her back."

Cilla made a tutting sound. "Alice was crazy about Zachariah, but she'd also had crushes on several other young men in our circle in the past. Being her older sister, I felt it was my duty to rein her in, since back then it was real easy to have your reputation tarnished. In an effort to dissuade her from making a fool of herself over Zachariah, I said some harsh things to her that I feel incredibly guilty about." Cilla bowed her head. "In my heart, I was trying to protect Alice, but she didn't see it that way. When she left Alaska, Alice made it pretty clear she wanted nothing to do with any of us."

"And you never heard from her again?" Annie asked. As loving as Gram had always been, she couldn't imagine that a rift could have kept her from her family for so many years.

Cilla dabbed tears away from her eyes. "There were a few postcards and letters over the years. And a few baby pictures of your mother. But we were led to believe she had gotten married to someone in New Hampshire. You have to remember, Annie, that having a child out of wedlock during that time would have been considered quite scandalous. She kept that secret all those years. And kept away from Love in the process."

"I give you my word, Annie," Zachariah said in a raspy voice. "I never knew Alice was pregnant when she left Alaska. She led me to believe that she was leaving to marry a pen pal she had been corresponding with. I was sad about it, but considering the way I had treated her, I had no right to stop her."

Eli walked up and grabbed Cilla's hand. "In the end, Zachariah never did marry. He's been an eternal bachelor all of these years."

Annie looked over at Zachariah. "Would you have married Gram if she had stayed here?"

"I'd like to say yes to that question, but my whole life, I've had trouble wrapping my head around the idea of settling down. Who's to say what might have happened?" he said, his eyes blinking like an owl's.

"Do you think you have room in your life for a granddaughter?" she asked.

Zachariah's eyes filled with tears. "Oh, Annie. You have no idea how much room is in this old heart of mine."

Annie reached out and hugged Zachariah as the townsfolk broke into applause. Tears were streaming down her face, and she whispered, "Thank you for making my dream come true, Zachariah. I've always wanted a grandpa."

"Please call me Grampy. It would mean the world to me."

"Okay, Grampy," Annie said, nestling herself against his chest. Her heart swelled with joy at the notion that she did have a family here in Love. Not only a grandfather, but Aunt Cilla and Uncle Eli. And, she hoped, a cousin or two.

As the meeting was adjourned due to special circumstances, Annie found herself being led to the main hall by Declan. He pulled her behind a tall white column and pressed a dizzying kiss against her lips.

"I'm not sure if I made it clear in there, but I love you, Annie," Declan said. "I'm crazy about you."

Annie let out a sigh. "I love you, too, Declan. Thank you for showing up tonight and laying it all on the table. I needed that huge push off the ledge." She bowed her head. "I think I also needed to know that you were on my side." Her eyes were moist with tears. "And you showed me that quite convincingly."

"I'll always be on your side." He stroked her cheek with his thumb. "I'm sorry about last night. I don't need to protect the Prescotts. From now on, you're my main priority, Annie. Without you, my life isn't half as interesting. You bring everything into sharp focus. Suddenly I can see my future, and it's not this big old blank slate. It's in vivid color, all reds and purples with big swirls and curlicues."

"Loving you has made me stronger," Annie said. "You've helped me live out my motto of living courageously, Declan. And you've helped me find my roots. And not just a grandfather. I have an aunt. And Eli is my uncle. And there are probably cousins, too," she gushed.

"Settle down, Annie. There will be plenty of time to figure all that out," Declan said with a grin. "I have a present for you." He reached down behind the column and pulled out a box.

"Open it," Declan instructed. "I ordered it right after our adventure in Chugach National Forest. I've been waiting for the right moment to spring it on you."

"What's inside?" Annie asked as she eyed the prettily wrapped package.

Declan resembled the cat who had swallowed the cream. "You have to open it to find out," he teased.

With the eagerness of a child on her birthday, Annie began to rip open the package. Within seconds, gift wrap and ribbons were everywhere. Annie let out a squeal as she gazed upon her present. "It's a copy of *Under a Dark Moon*, Leslie Lemon's first book. There are only a few hundred copies of this in existence." She pressed it against her chest and heaved a tremendous sigh. Tears slid down her face. "How on earth did you do this? It must have cost a small fortune."

"Hey! What's with the waterworks? I have a pilot friend who has connections with the European publisher of that gem. He owed me a favor. When I saw how brave you were when we crash-landed, I knew that I wanted to do something special for you." Declan appeared to be bursting with satisfaction at being able to make her happy. His over-the-top grin was contagious.

Annie smiled. "Other than Gram, I've never had anyone in my life care enough about me to do something like this. I've never had anyone know me so well, so completely as to understand my heart's desires."

Declan dipped his head and placed a firm kiss on her lips. He cupped her face between his palms and murmured her name as the kiss ended. "Well, you've got me now, and I'm not going anywhere, sweetheart. You're stuck with me."

Annie couldn't stop looking at the book. "It's amazing, Declan. I love it."

"And I love you, Annie. More than I ever imagined it was possible to love another human being. Before you came into my world, I was convinced that love wasn't meant for me. I was half the man I am today, stumbling around in the dark and allowing the past to threaten my future. Our future."

"Ours?" Annie squeaked. Her eyes went wide, and she began to blink fast and furiously.

"Open the book," he urged. "I put a little something in there on the way over here."

With trembling fingers, Annie opened the book and took out the note he had placed inside the front cover. She read it aloud. "Will you?" She swung her gaze up to look at him.

"Will I what?" she asked, her heart pounding as it dawned on her that her life was about to change in a monumental way.

* * *

Declan lowered himself to one knee. He dug inside his pocket and pulled out a wooden ring box. He flipped it open to reveal a sparkling ring. He looked up at Annie, and with his heart thumping wildly in his chest, said the four words he never imagined would ever come out of his mouth. "Will you marry me?" Annie covered her mouth with one hand while clutching the book in the other.

"Will I? Of course I will," she said, throwing her arms around his neck and smothering him with kisses. When she finally let go of him, Declan held up the ring.

"Annie. This is a pretty old-fashioned ring. It's been sitting in my sock drawer for years and years. It belonged to my mother. It has a lot of sentimental meaning, so I hope you love it as much as she always did."

"You know I love vintage things, Declan." He placed the ring on her finger as she let out a gasp of appreciation. "It's stunning, Declan. And I'm honored to wear your mother's ring."

"Thank you for loving me, Annie," Declan said, tears forming in his eyes. "This proposal might be a bit spur-of-the-moment, but the love I feel for you is anything but. It's solid and grounded."

"Loving you was my destiny," Annie said. "I never thought you and I would be a match. But we are. As perfect a match as there ever could be," she chirped.

"Right here, right now, I want to kiss you, Annie Murray. To celebrate our big news."

"Oh, really," she said in a sassy voice. "Is that a promise?"

"Without question," he murmured as he placed his

lips over hers and dipped her backward in a kiss that heralded their glorious future and the joy they had found in each other's arms.

Epilogue

Annie stood on the front steps of the Free Library of Love and breathed in the crisp wintry air. It was a frigid December morning, but she was almost oblivious to the low temperature and the winter wonderland all around her. All she wanted to do was make her way inside the library so she could see Declan decked out in his Sunday best. She was getting married today. Her beautiful rhinestone-encrusted wedding dress with the lace at the cuffs had been a wonderful discovery at a vintage store in Anchorage. It was her dream dress for her fairy-tale wedding to the love of her life.

"Ready to go inside?" Zachariah asked. "If you want to make a run for it, I've got a getaway car." Her grandfather was dressed in an old-fashioned gray topper. He had decorated his cane to match the cranberry accents of her wedding party.

Annie nodded. Although her throat felt clogged with emotion, there was something resting on her heart that she needed to share with her grandfather. Moisture was already gathering in her eyes as she turned toward him.

"Grampy. I just want to tell you that finding you has changed me. Knowing that I have family ties here in Love makes all the difference in the world to me. You're one of the biggest reasons that I feel I belong here. And even though we haven't known each other very long, I love you very much."

Zachariah reached out and clasped her hand in his. He squeezed it tightly. "I wish I'd known you all your life, but I'm still grateful that you came looking for me. Any man would be proud to claim you. You're an extraordinary woman, just like your Gram."

Tears slid down Annie's face. For so long, she had wanted to hear those words from a male figure in her life. Knowing that Zachariah had stepped up to claim her and to be a part of her life had allowed her to put to rest the shadows in her family tree. The cycle had been broken. And now, she could embrace her future with Declan with not a single reservation about the past. Her groom had also put a lid on his painful family history. By coming to terms with the tragedy of his mother's death and his father's downward spiral, Declan had opened a window for their glorious future. There wasn't a single thing holding them back.

"I'm ready to become Mrs. Declan O'Rourke," she announced as a calm feeling swept over her. Once they stepped inside the library, Sophie and Hazel were there waiting for them in the foyer. Both women were dressed in cranberry-colored bridesmaid's dresses. Sophie's dress stopped right below the knee, while Hazel's swept all the way to her ankles. They each reached out and hugged Annie, murmuring words of encouragement and blessings.

"I hope Jasper gets some inspiration from all these

weddings popping up around him," Hazel cracked. "I'm not getting any younger."

"You'd make a lovely bride at any age," Sophie said, patting Hazel on the shoulder.

"Remember to tell Jasper that at the reception," Hazel urged. "He needs all the encouragement he can get. The old coot is beginning to take me for granted."

The doors of the grand room were flung wide open, signaling that it was time for the wedding to start. Side by side, Hazel and Sophie began to walk across the threshold and down the flower-strewn aisle.

A hush fell over the crowd as the wedding march rang out in the main hall. Zachariah held out his arm, and they began to slowly walk into the room. Annie smiled as she looked at all the books sitting proudly on the shelves. A feeling of pride swelled inside her. This place was a testament to the future of this town. Generations of townsfolk would benefit from the library's extensive catalog. Encyclopedias. Travel books. Stories about kings and queens and faraway places. Books that would fuel imaginations and encourage thinking and dreaming and aspiring.

Annie sucked in a breath at the sight of her groom. Dressed in his midnight-blue tux, a crisp white shirt and a cranberry-colored bow tie, he looked spectacular. Swoon-worthy. Boone stood right by his side, while Finn, Cameron and Liam were behind them. She had to smile as Declan fidgeted impatiently with his collar. He had gotten dressed up for her. Knowing Declan, he would have cheerfully worn his leather aviator jacket and jeans to the ceremony.

Once he caught sight of her walking down the aisle, his gaze never strayed from her. Although Annie knew the room was packed with dozens of well-wishers and friends, all she saw was Declan. Her hero. The man who would always own her heart.

Before she was even halfway down the aisle, Declan began rushing toward her. He stopped beside her, his grin as wide as the ocean.

"I'm sorry. I couldn't wait a second longer," Declan said. He moved to her left side and linked their hands together. They continued to walk down the aisle until Zachariah handed Annie over to Declan, then took his seat in the front row.

"Eager to marry this amazing woman, aren't you?" Pastor Jack Teagan teased, his eyes alight with merriment.

"Imagine that," Declan drawled. "Just shows you what the love of a good woman can do."

Pastor Jack began the ceremony. "We are gathered here today to celebrate the blessed union of Declan O'Rourke and Annie Murray, a couple who has made the decision to walk through life together."

Annie could barely hold back the tide of tears as she listened to the pastor's words. After a few minutes he turned toward Declan. "I'm going to hand things over to you now. I know you have prepared your vows to Annie, as she has for you."

Declan reached for Annie's hand and began reciting his vows. "Before you came to town, I was pretty convinced I would be single for the rest of my days." Tears gathered in his eyes. "Sometimes the past can make us think we're not worthy of good things. I was afraid to hope, Annie. You showed me that everything I have ever wanted was right there within reach. I just had to believe. And now I want to make sure all your dreams come true. I vow to spend the rest of my life by your side."

Annie smiled at her groom through a haze of tears. "Declan, I thought you were a hero right from the start. You denied it, but I always knew you were. You made me feel safe when we were stranded out there in the wilderness. And you've been making me feel that way ever since. After Gram died, I didn't have a place that felt like home. Until you. You make me feel as if I'm right where I belong. Where God always intended me to be."

Pastor Jack continued the service and pronounced Declan and Annie husband and wife. As they exchanged their first kiss as a married couple, both the bride and groom rejoiced in the fact that the darkness of the past had been stamped out by their beautiful present.

They were blessed with the knowledge that they would be living out their lives in love.

* * * * *

If you enjoyed this visit to Love, Alaska, pick up the other stories in the ALASKAN GROOMS *series by Belle Calhoune.*

AN ALASKAN WEDDING
ALASKAN REUNION

Available now from Love Inspired!
Find more great reads at www.LoveInspired.com

Dear Reader,

Thank you for joining me on this voyage to Love, Alaska. I hope you enjoyed reading Declan and Annie's story. Writing this book was a joyful experience. There's nothing more fascinating than seeing two people fall in love despite their best intentions to resist the pull in that direction.

Both Declan and Annie have a hole inside them that needs to be filled up. The hurts of the past loom large for both of them and play an important part in their romantic lives. Annie doesn't want to repeat the cycle of single mothers in her family, while Declan doesn't believe he's worthy of a happy ending. Annie yearns to find a soft place to fall. Declan wants things he can't even dare to hope for. Somehow, with a little help from faith and true love, they find hope in each other's arms.

Being an author is my dream job. My daughter once told me that I was one of the lucky few who actually get to work in the profession of their dreams. I feel very blessed. It never gets old to see my books in print. Writing for Love Inspired is an honor.

It's always delightful to hear from readers. You can reach me by email at scalhoune@gmail.com, at my Author Belle Calhoune Facebook page, on my website, bellecalhoune.com, or on Twitter @BelleCalhoune.

Blessings,
Belle

REQUEST YOUR FREE BOOKS!

2 FREE INSPIRATIONAL NOVELS
PLUS 2
FREE
MYSTERY GIFTS

Love Inspired®

YES! Please send me 2 FREE Love Inspired® novels and my 2 FREE mystery gifts (gifts are worth about $10). After receiving them, if I don't wish to receive any more books, I can return the shipping statement marked "cancel." If I don't cancel, I will receive 6 brand-new novels every month and be billed just $4.99 per book in the U.S. or $5.49 per book in Canada. That's a saving of at least 17% off the cover price. It's quite a bargain! Shipping and handling is just 50¢ per book in the U.S. and 75¢ per book in Canada.* I understand that accepting the 2 free books and gifts places me under no obligation to buy anything. I can always return a shipment and cancel at any time. Even if I never buy another book, the two free books and gifts are mine to keep forever.

105/305 IDN GH5P

Name	(PLEASE PRINT)

Address		Apt. #

City	State/Prov.	Zip/Postal Code

Signature (if under 18, a parent or guardian must sign)

Mail to the **Reader Service:**
IN U.S.A.: P.O. Box 1867, Buffalo, NY 14240-1867
IN CANADA: P.O. Box 609, Fort Erie, Ontario L2A 5X3

**Are you a subscriber to Love Inspired® books
and want to receive the larger-print edition?
Call 1-800-873-8635 or visit www.ReaderService.com.**

* Terms and prices subject to change without notice. Prices do not include applicable taxes. Sales tax applicable in N.Y. Canadian residents will be charged applicable taxes. Offer not valid in Quebec. This offer is limited to one order per household. Not valid for current subscribers to Love Inspired books. All orders subject to credit approval. Credit or debit balances in a customer's account(s) may be offset by any other outstanding balance owed by or to the customer. Please allow 4 to 6 weeks for delivery. Offer available while quantities last.

Your Privacy—The Reader Service is committed to protecting your privacy. Our Privacy Policy is available online at www.ReaderService.com or upon request from the Reader Service.

We make a portion of our mailing list available to reputable third parties that offer products we believe may interest you. If you prefer that we not exchange your name with third parties, or if you wish to clarify or modify your communication preferences, please visit us at www.ReaderService.com/consumerschoice or write to us at Reader Service Preference Service, P.O. Box 9062, Buffalo, NY 14240-9062. Include your complete name and address.

LII5

When a handsome Amish mill owner breaks his leg, a feisty young Amish woman agrees to be his housekeeper. But will two weeks together lead to romance or heartbreak?

Read on for a sneak preview of
A BEAU FOR KATIE,
the third book in Emma Miller's miniseries
THE AMISH MATCHMAKER.

"Here's Katie," Sara the matchmaker announced. "She'll lend a hand with the housework until you're back on your feet." She motioned Katie to approach the bed. "I think you two already know each other."

"*Ya,*" Freeman admitted gruffly. "We do."

Katie removed her black bonnet. Freeman Kemp wasn't hard on the eyes. Even lying flat in a bed, one leg in a cast, he was still a striking figure of a man. The pain lines at the corners of his mouth couldn't hide his masculine jaw. His wavy brown hair badly needed a haircut, and he had at least a week's growth of dark beard, but the cotton undershirt revealed broad, muscular shoulders and arms.

Freeman's compelling gaze met hers. His eyes were brown, almost amber, with darker swirls of color. Unnerved, she uttered in a hushed tone, "Good morning, Freeman."

Then Katie turned away to inspect the kitchen that would be her domain for the next two weeks. She'd never been inside the house before, but from the outside, she'd thought it was beautiful. Now, standing in the spacious kitchen, she liked it even more. The only thing that looked out of place was the bed containing the frowning Freeman.

"You must be in a lot of pain," Sara remarked, gently patting Freeman's cast.

"*Ne*. Nothing to speak of."

Katie nodded. "Well, rest and proper food for an invalid will do you the most good."

Freeman glanced away. "I'm *not* an invalid."

Katie sighed. If your leg encased in a cast didn't make you an invalid, she didn't know what did. But Freeman, as she recalled, had a stubborn nature.

For an eligible bachelor who owned a house, a mill and two hundred acres of prime land to remain single into his midthirties was almost unheard of among the Amish. Add to that, Freeman's rugged good looks. It made him the catch of the county. They could have him. She was not a giggling teenager who could be swept off her feet by a pretty face. Working in his house for two whole weeks wasn't going to be easy, but he didn't intimidate her. She'd told Sara she'd take the job and she was a woman of her word.

Don't miss
A BEAU FOR KATIE by Emma Miller,
available August 2016 wherever
Love Inspired® books and ebooks are sold.

www.LoveInspired.com

SPECIAL EXCERPT FROM

Love Inspired HISTORICAL

With her uncle trying to claim her ranch, widow
Lula May Barlow has no time to worry about romance.
But can she resist Edmund McKay—the handsome
cowboy next door—when he helps her fight for her
land…and when her children start playing matchmaker?

Read on for a sneak preview of
A FAMILY FOR THE RANCHER,
the heartwarming continuation of the series
LONE STAR COWBOY LEAGUE:
THE FOUNDING YEARS

"Just wanted to return your book."

Book?

Lula May saw her children slinking out of the barn,
guilty looks on their faces. So that's why they'd made such
nuisances of themselves out at the pasture. They'd wanted
her to send them off to play so they could take the book to
Edmund. And she knew exactly why. Those little rascals
were full-out matchmaking! Casting a look at Edmund,
she faced the inevitable, which wasn't really all that bad.
"Will you come in for coffee?"

He tilted his hat back to reveal his broad forehead, where
dark blond curls clustered and made him look younger
than his thirty-three years. "Coffee would be good."

Lula May led him in through the back door. To her
horror, Uncle sat at the kitchen table hungrily eyeing
the cake she'd made for Edmund…and almost forgotten
about. Now she'd have no excuse for not introducing them
before she figured out how to get rid of Floyd.

"Edmund, this is Floyd Jones." She forced herself to add,
"My uncle. Floyd, this is my neighbor, Edmund McKay."

As the children had noted last week when Edmund first

stepped into her kitchen, he took up a good portion of the room. Even Uncle seemed a bit unsettled by his presence. While the men chatted about the weather, however, Lula May could see the old wiliness and false charm creeping into Uncle's words and facial expressions. She recognized the old man's attempt to figure Edmund out so he could control him.

Pauline and Daniel worked at the sink, urgent whispers going back and forth. Why had they become so bold in their matchmaking? Was it possible they sensed the danger of Uncle's presence and wanted to lure Edmund over here to protect her? She wouldn't have any of that. She'd find a solution without any help from anybody, especially not her neighbor. Her only regret was that she hadn't been able to protect the children from realizing Uncle wasn't a good man. If she could have found a way to be nicer to him… No, that wasn't possible. Not when he'd come here for the distinct purpose of seizing everything she owned.

The men enjoyed their coffee and cake, after which Edmund suggested they take a walk around the property to build up an appetite for supper.

"We'd like to go for a walk with you, Mr. McKay," Pauline said. "May we, Mama?"

Lula May hesitated. Let them continue their matchmaking or make them spend time with Uncle? Neither option pleased her. When had she lost control of her household? About a week before Uncle arrived, that was when, the day when Edmund had walked into her kitchen and invited himself into her…or rather, her eldest son's life.

"You may go, but don't pester Mr. McKay." She gave the children a narrow-eyed look of warning.

Their innocent blinks did nothing to reassure her.

Don't miss
A FAMILY FOR THE RANCHER
by Louise M. Gouge, available August 2016 wherever
Love Inspired® Historical books and ebooks are sold.

www.LoveInspired.com

LIHEXP0716